For Rory,
whom I've never even met.

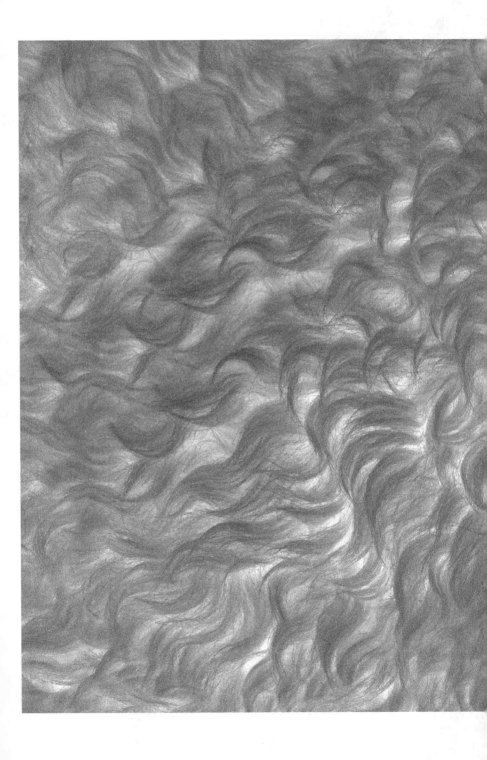

Creomoxxie Tales

Via Dyri

Persephone Jayne

Creomoxxie Tales

Via Dyri

Persephone Jayne

Chapter heading art is reproduced from and used with the permission of:
© Asmodee Group. All rights reserved.
Rory's Story Cubes is a trademark of Asmodee Group

ShitshitshitSSSSSHHHHHHhiiiii- *What am
I even doing here? I need a drink.*

I patted myself down, looking for my flask. I
found my phone tucked into my hip pocket, but
where was my drink?

Wynn, my ride, stepped over and around the
guards' twisted limbs, causing me to rock back
and forth as we crossed the bridge.

Wynn kicked her right back leg a bit, and I
remembered my flask was in the saddlebag. I
dug it out, which was helpful because I was still
trying to make sense of what I'd just seen.

Pinky, the fairy, had literally taken sticks
from the ground and carved them quickly and
efficiently. Then, when the conversation with the
guards turned to fighting… Pinky, armed only
with the nun-chucks she'd just carved, took

them out. Both guards. I mean, she IS our 'weapons master', but honestly? I had assumed that was a satirical misnomer. She's literally pink, dainty as any fairy I've ever met, and has a soft lilting voice and bouncy pink locks.

What am I even for? Seriously.

I have no skills even close to that. I doubt anyone on this quest is going to need a chai latte with a shot of patience. Well, maybe Flora.

I took a swig from my flask and let the whiskey warm my belly while the anti-anxiety shot calmed my spirit. I knew the last minute inspiration to spell my drink was a good idea.

Wynn snorted as we touched ground on the other side of the bridge.

Was she laughing at me?

I wondered again at her scraggly appearance. In the group of six unicorns we were riding, she was the only one who looked like... her. The rest were bright, colorful, tall llamas with horns sticking from the middle of their heads. Mine was none of those things.

Her fur, despite looking like a shaggy blue grey dog, was softer than any goat I'd ever encountered and when I said as much, she bucked me off in front of the entire crew. That was day one and the bruise on my ass now reminds me with every bump that she is not a goat. She is a unicorn.

I also understand that she's not *mine*. She is a hired hand, just like me.

It's her horn that is most interesting though. Right above her left eye, it twists up from her head where the other's horns are straight. Wynn's horn starts blue grey, like her fur, and then fades to an inky black tip. I'm pretty certain it sparkles, like constellations in the night sky of my childhood, but no one else sees it. I know this because they looked at me like I'd lost my mind when I mentioned it. Wynn also smells like bananas and sugar. I wasn't about to mention that after the 'horn revelation'. Flora, the leader of our little quest, has assured me that my ride is the most powerful unicorn she's ever met. But I'm pretty sure it's only these six unicorns that she can count as having met, so I'm not putting too much stock in her claim just yet.

"We'll head a little further and camp outside the Fold tonight. Then tomorrow? It's into Volarmaa," Flora announced without looking back.

I turned and checked. We all made it across the bridge. Even the empty unicorn that Flora assures me has an occupant, was now walking along behind me.

3

Flora Moonweb. You might expect, with a name like that, she'd be tall, with skin as soft as a flower and hair like moonbeams. You'd be wrong. She's a troll. I'm not talking gruff personality like a troll or dumb as a box of rocks like a troll. No. Actually, a troll. She claims to be a fairy cursed into that form. But, really, if I had a dime for every- no, wait, dimes are from the fictional realm. If I had a loot for every shaggy looking shrew claiming to be cursed? Anyway, I believe that as much as I believe my unicorn is the most powerful in the bunch. If you recall, that's not a lot.

So why do I follow her? Meh. It's nice to have a quest, even if it is fake. It's better than listening to the Three Sisters, who own the coffee shop, blabbering on about the state of the realms and the need for unification, which I really think they mean as human realm domination. Plus, I've worked there for over 2 years without a raise, it was time to go. A paying gig that asked me to travel? Yeah, I was in.

"Wait. Did you say the Fold?" I asked, raising up in my seat to be heard.

"I did, Alta," Flora hollered, still not turning back. "How else did you think we're going to get to the Fairy Realm?"

"Aren't we were already IN Volarmaa? Right? We crossed the Briass River two days ago. We skirted the Living Forest, and we just passed Mossgate, which I know is a Volarmaa city."

"Alta, you really haven't left the Human Realm in a while," Pinky said, trotting her unicorn up beside me. "You, as this size, are in Volarmaa… but the fairies exist on a different plane… in our right size. The Fold changes us so we can interact with the rest of Creomoxxie."

"I thought the Fold was an old wives' tale," I said, mostly to myself.

Pinky laughed and rode ahead. Making my comment so ridiculous, it didn't even warrant an explanation.

"What do wives, young or old, have to do with it?" Wynn's voice, gruff and scratchy, said in my brain. I had, of course, expected a light, lilting, airy, cloudy, rainbow kind of voice. She was a unicorn, after all. But her voice sounded like her fur looked rough, grey and raspy.

"It's just a saying."

"The Human Realm is so weird."

"It's not from Embri."

I ignored Wynn's next question and shouted to the front again, "I thought the Fold was a myth."

"How do you think I got here, Alta?" Flora said, shouting into the air so she didn't have to turn around and face me. "Why did you think Pinky and I aren't flying?"

Honestly, I was skeptical of the validity of this quest... so I literally hadn't considered how Flora got here. Or that two members of our team were fairies, but had yet to fly. I assumed it was all proof of a bogus quest. I left it. Not really wanting to make myself the only idiot who joins a quest they don't even believe is real. That's definitely a status of looser I didn't want this group labeling me with.

"Don't underestimate yourself," Wynn laughed in my head, *"I have faith you'll be 'loser', labeled soon enough."*

I ignored that too. I didn't want to be fighting with the one Creomoxxian responsible for getting me around right now. Plus, knowing exactly what she thought of me, through a telepathic link, was a bit much for my brain to process.

Instead, I rode in silence, taking in the realm.

Volarmaa, well, this version of it anyway- version? Plain? Pre-fold? Whatever it's called, it's far more lush than Embri. The Human Realm is mostly dirt. Dry and dusty, it gags at your throat, leaving you in a constant state of thirst. But this...

Trees towered over us as we had woven in and out of mountains and hills. The twin suns shone down, but the shade of the canopy protected us from their rays. Light dappled on Wynn's fur as we walked, and I imagined her sparkling like a unicorn from my father's realm.

"Horses," Wynn said, making no attempt to hide her disgust.

"What's wrong with a horse being a unicorn?"

"Ha!" She barked a fake laugh at me. *"Horses are only worth the height their legs afford them for reaching upper shelves... which! they need because none of them have ever been born a unicorn."*

"Well, in my father's realm, unicorns are always depicted as being horses with horns."

"That's the biggest false advertising campaign ever. They duped an entire realm into believing that?"

"Oh, no one actually believes unicorns are real."

Wynn went silent.

"Sorry."

No reply.

After crossing the bridge, we had come out of the forest surrounding Mossgate, and slowly descended a mountainous cliff side. The vast ocean below had me thinking back to my father's realm. I had visited the ocean, once in

Jersey, and a few times in Florida. Those were nothing compared to this. The ocean in Creomoxxie was a brilliant blue against the pale lavender sky and I could have sworn that I saw sea creatures swimming below its surface. It's that clear. Wynn said I was imagining things. I ignored her.

We came close to the river's mouth, sea spray hitting my nose and gagging my throat while simultaneously stinging my eyes. Was the ocean this fishy in my childhood? The river we had crossed, and then descended along, emptied into the ocean at the bottom of the cliff and I realized there was no bridge. I wondered how Flora planned to get us across.

"That's why we're here," Wynn answered my thought.

"So you're talking to me again? And I really need you to stop listening to my thoughts all day."

"I'm not listening, so much as you're thinking."

"I'm what?"

"Thinking. So. Loud." Wynn retorted.

"How are you planning to help with this?" I asked, more annoyance in my voice than I had intended.

"I guess you'll see." Wynn gave me a mental shrug, and I rolled my eyes, hoping she wouldn't buck me off again. This narrow, cliff side trail, above a churning ocean, was no place I'd survive a fall.

"Alright." Flora called as we reached the ocean, "Elgar, are the unicorns ready?" The empty unicorn huffed and stomped his hooves. Which I took to mean yes, because Flora turned to the rest of us, "Hold on tight. I don't need to lose anyone into the churning ocean."

"I'm sorry. Hold on to what?" I asked no one in particular.

"Me," Wynn said before taking off into the air.

2

Me? Crazy? I should get off this
unicorn and slap whoever said that.
Now mount up. The realm of fairies
is unpredictable and getting in can be," Flora
said the next morning as we prepared to Fold.
She paused for dramatic effect. That was the
first thing I learned about Flora, dramatic flair.
"Well, frankly? It can be a bitch." She surveyed
the lot of us, daring someone to argue.

I knew that tactic. My old bosses used it
daily.

Luckily, no one in this group was dumb
enough to fall for it. I immediately thought of
the newest barista, who just had to run her
mouth and make the morning meeting
agonizingly longer than it needed to be. No.
These Creomoxxians shut their traps and moved
on. For the millionth time since doing so, I was

glad to have left the dead end coffee shop. Even if the quest turned out to be the fake I expected.

The flight on the unicorns, over the churning ocean, had been all my little brain could handle. I made my camp along with the others and fell asleep fast, thankful for having made it across safely. Wynn had mumbled a few things about trusting her abilities more... but I ignored them. The idea of Folding today... after flying over the ocean yesterday... sleep had been more urgent than arguing with Wynn over how much of my life I trusted her with.

I want to believe Flora... and Pinky, about the Fold. But really? No one had actually been through it in ages. Decades? Who knows... that's how myths get created. No one knows the truth of it.

Flora had led us this far, but if 'the Fold' ends up being that circle of elm trees over there, I won't exactly be surprised. I spurred my goat, I mean, unicorn, into line following the rest. She stands two heads shorter than any of the others, their long llama necks dwarfing her, accentuating the difference in height.

Flora leads the pack- yep! You guessed it! To the circle of elms. I again question my decision to leave the coffee house counter and join this quest. Yeah, it's that kind of flippy-floppy emotional rollercoaster of a trip. Flora and her unicorn enter the circle and wait. Huffing, tapping her foot in the air beside Grable's belly. The unicorn doesn't seem to mind. Flora, sighing loudly, made no attempt to hide her impatience while the rest of us slowly filed into the circle.

"Alta! Come on," Flora shouted at me.

I considered telling her I have no control over the unicorn I ride... but I kept my mouth shut. I learned my lesson from the coffee house staff meetings.

"It will be nice to be my right size again," Pinky said. She's the only fairy on the crew, not counting Flora, the fake troll fairy. Pinky is half as tall as her unicorn and her skin is as milky pale pink as the animal's fluffy fur. They look like two pink peas in a sweet pink pod. Pinky and her unicorn have been together since they were bouncing babes. I've gathered, anyway, from the way they work so well together.

"Is there a doorway? Or what?" Celairil called from behind me. She's an elf and our... engineer, I guess. She stands a head over me and her pitch black skin stands in contrast to her Anda, which is bright yellow and glows faintly, like, all the time. Making her seem angelic as we gather outside the fairy realm. Her yellow hair flows down her back like a bundle of vines in a rainforest to her knees. It's usually pulled into a massive braid, which I have noticed is convenient for quick maneuvers. I wish I could braid my hair out of my face like that. I hate looking clumsy. But I hate my ears even more. So the hair stays down.

I pulled Wynn into her spot in the circle. Pull is a strong word. I rest my hands in my lap or tangle fingers in her fur a bit and she goes where she goes. She's not my pet or my friend, she's made that clear.

Erasto flashes me a smile as we fall into line. He's tall and sweet smelling, for a dwarf. He also has a wit that no one else seems to get. Maybe it's my fictional half. I enjoyed riding near him. Time passes better when you can laugh.

Wynn's gruff voice interrupted my inner monologue with a few teasing noises.

"Stop listening to my thoughts," I whisper through clinched teeth into her ear.

The last, 'non-empty' unicorn filed into place and Flora addressed us all, as regally as a troll can.

"Hold on to your knickers. This is going to suck."

What kind of pep talk was that?

Before I could answer myself, I was yanked off Wynn and flung into the air. I grabbed wildly at her fur, to avoid losing her but also to avoid

losing me. My brain went fuzzy, and my body
felt as if it was burning and freezing at the same
time. Like that time I was sick and had to go to
the hospital and they realized my appendix had
burst. Yes. It felt exactly like that except all over
my body.

And then it stopped. I felt like I was floating.
No wait- falling, I was falling! I flailed my arms
in an attempt to, what, fly? No time to consider
because that's when I realized I couldn't see
anything. I'm not sure if my eyes weren't
working or if it's just that dark here. Here.
Where are we? Wait. I stopped falling. Wynn
nudged my arm and my hand felt grass under
me. She didn't hate me nearly as much as I
thought. Or she has no choice but to check on
me because she's being paid... whatever it is you
pay unicorns. Either way, I'm grateful and I gave
her a pat.

"Wynn, where are we?" I asked, pulling my
hand from her head and rubbing my eyes as they
adjusted to the light. A grunt of disgust entered
my brain as my entire body stiffened at the
feeling of her voice in my head. Like suddenly,
her voice was a mountain shoving itself into my
skull. More like the first time she'd spoken to
me telepathically.

"The fairy realm. I hate it here. Everything's
so," she searched for the right word, "little."

14

"Little?" I echoed, trying to shake the sand paper feeling from my brain and looking around to see what she meant. Everything actually looked big. The grass I had just been sitting on was taller than I was. The smell of earth was pungent.

"Everyone make it?" Flora asked, but from where I couldn't tell. Her voice seemed to come from everywhere. "Up here," she said as if in exact answer to my internal question. I looked up and there, hovering above me was Flora, the troll. Only she had big, bright wings. Fairy wings, I guess. Cursed, indeed. I heard rustling to my left and saw Stone come into view through the grasses.

Sworn to protect the FairyTroll on her quest. I guess that made Stone 'the muscle'. And muscle he is. His arm is as big around as my head. His shirt was ripped in various places, I'm sure, from flexing. If I'd have met him under regular circumstances… well, I probably would have gawked, said something idiotic, then tripped down some stairs… but still. Who knew I could be into trolls?

I smiled at him and tried to wave, but my hand wouldn't move. Why wouldn't my hand move? I looked down at it asking myself the question again. Wynn must have heard me thinking in panic, 'cause she sniffed it. I tried picking it up with my other hand and couldn't feel it. I was watching my right hand hold my left and my left felt nothing.

"I can't feel my hand!" I screamed. Running up to Flora in my panic. "I can't feel my hand!"

"Well, Erasto has arrived with his eyes in backwards. And the Elves are nowhere to be seen. Your little hand problem will have to wait," she yelled at me. "Celairil! Thank the Duster! Is Hemlock with you?"

Her voice got distant as she flew to where she was needed. Stone was staring at me. Great. I had screamed like a banshee about my hand and he had heard it. And seen me. Now he was silently judging me for it. He walked closer, I'm sure, to poke fun at my horrible injury. He reached for my arm.

Here it comes.

"Lemme see." He spoke so softly that I almost had to ask him to repeat. But his outstretched hand gave me permission to shove my hand into his. I wasn't going to interrupt my intimate contact with Mr. Muscles by asking questions. I picked my left arm up with my right and held it out. He took it. Man! I wish I could feel my arm right now. He started rubbing his hands up and down my arm.

Please don't faint. Please don't faint- those birds sound so chipper. Focus. Don't faint.

16

"It's just numb from the magical shrink. Common side effect." I could feel my entire arm now, my hand and my fingers, thanks to his rubbing. "Can you feel anything yet?" I shook my head. The weirdo, half Fictional girl, hadn't had much luck with romance in Creomoxxie, go figure. This might be the last time someone this burley touched me, ever. I wasn't even actually interested in Stone. He was just so... muscle-y. You bet I'm milking it. He rubbed a while longer, then let go. I smiled again and managed a mumbled 'thanks' before he walked away.

"He knew you were lying," came Wynn's gruffness in my brain. I shot her a look of innocence. *"He may be mostly Troll, but somewhere there was human on that family tree. He can sense your feelings when he's touching you."* I looked at her with raised eyebrows and twisted my lips. No way that was true. I'm mostly human and I can't do that... wait, can I? No. My dad, being fictional human and not Creomoxxian human, probably snuffed that out. Thanks Dad.

3

W ait! Did he say magical shrink?" I asked Wynn. She had no response, so I yelled after Stone. "What does that mean? Magical shrink?" Chasing him to catch up. Wynn on my heels, not willing to answer me but, I guess curious what answers I got. Stone stopped and turned to look at me.

"How else did you expect to get into the realm of fairies?" He asked.

"Honestly? I wasn't completely sold on the whole 'quest to break a curse' thing. So I wasn't expecting to actually 'cross realms', or whatever." He looked at me and I knew again he was judging me. "I know. Who joins a quest they don't even believe in?" I said for him, turning to walk away without my answers.

"I was actually wondering if I've met you somewhere before." I turned back and his gaze bore into mine. I felt like I should cover up with a blanket or build a cinder block bunker around myself. His brown eyes, I realized, were flecked with red and yellow. Like a fire. A fire that was now looking into my soul.

"Stop," I finally said. "We've never met. I would have remembered you," I promised him. No one is forgetting the giant troll with purple hair and literal stones growing over his chest instead of hair.

"Still. Something about your hair in the breeze and the rays of the setting suns... It's familiar." His voice trailed off as he ran his hands through the air, tracing the rays he was talking of.

I blushed. And hoped the sunset was covering it well enough.

"Now! Who was it that called this quest crazy?" Flora asked as she dismounted Grable, who shot outside the circle of elms like a dwarf out of the bathhouse- I shouldn't say that. Erasto is the cleanest quest mate I have- We all sort of looked at each other. No one was about to take responsibility if we could avoid it. Truth was? We'd all called it crazy at some point. Called *her* crazy. "Well it IS," Flora went on. "Crazy in every possible way. Getting cursed." She threw her arm around herself in a dramatic flurry. "Getting out of the fairy realm with Stone. Finding all of you to help me on my quest. Getting the lot of you back into the fairy realm?" She dropped her thick body onto a clump of grass and started digging next to it. "Crazy? Yes! And Not easy. Let me tell you. So let's just find a place to camp so we can get on with reversing the curse, and everyone can go back to their normal lives and I can properly pummel the prince."

I leaned over to Wynn, asking, "The prince?" Wynn snorted and galloped off to follow Grable.

"What IS the plan?" Celairil asked.

"Cel," Flora huffed and burrowed her backside into the shallow hole she'd dug. "I'm just so tired." And she fell straight to sleep. Snoring and drooling as if she had been for hours. I watched Celairil for a clue of what to do next and found it when she started setting up camp. I went to pull my tarp and poles out of my pack and realized the pack was on Wynn, so I started off in the direction she had galloped. The grass was too high and I couldn't see where the unicorns went. I assumed they went together, jumped up to see over the grass, and felt something fluttering over my back. I turned and twisted my head around to see what it was and realized that the ground was no longer touching my feet.

Wings? I have wings.

Wings!

Have I always had them?

Definitely not.

I scooped my hands around my back to make sure I wasn't imagining them. They collapsed under my hands, which flopped me back to the ground.

Running to Stone, I shouted, "Wings too? Is that part of the magical shrink?"

He snapped his head up, and his eyes got wide. Giant fiery orbs resting under his perfectly bushy lavender eyebrows answer me. No. This is not part of the magical shrink.

"Flora! Get up!" He shouted toward her sleeping trollness. Flora shot up and flew over. Stone was already at my side, hand outstretched to grab my wings.

"Hey! Hands off." I swatted his hands away from my backside and turned so he couldn't grab them. He swatted me back and raised his eyebrows, questioning. I caved and turned so he could examine them.

"Told you this one was special," Flora whispered to Stone as they moved me around by my wings.

"Why do I have wings?!" I finally squeaked out, louder than I planned.

"No clue," Flora said. "It's literally never happened before, that I know of anyway. The only ones who have wings here are fairies. You must be part fairy. Congrats!" She slapped my back and her troll strength shoved me forward. I stumbled and Stone caught me before I hit the ground. Heat rushed to my cheeks, and I tossed my hair over my face to hide it.

He's just so close. I need to move. Move feet. Move.

He stood me up carefully, reaching a hand out to tuck my hair behind my ear. Tracing the slight point of it, he looked at me.

"Fictional on your Human side. Fairy, apparently. And…?" A step or two between us now, thanks to my finally moving feet, and I untuck the hair. "Special, indeed." Stone whispered as he walked past me, back toward his tent.

Flora was back at my wings now and putting me through a few paces. She asked me to flutter them, flap them, close them, fly around the grasses. During which, I saw the clearing everyone else was setting up in. Wynn was there, with the rest of the unicorns. I landed and Flora, satisfied with my abilities, headed back to her sleeping hole.

"Lucky you wore that top. Wings might have burst a regular shirt wide open," Flora said as she shimmied backward into her dugout.

I examined my shirt, feeling my way around the spaghetti straps at my back. They slid right on the outside of my new wings, allowing them to flow as needed.

"Flora, wait." Celairil called. "We must have a plan as we move forward. Now that we're back in the realm."

Flora yawned through her words, "The shrink takes it out of me. After a nap C. Promise."

4

Breakfast was tense, as Flora had slept all afternoon and all night. Celairil spent all her time pulling decisions out of Flora. Who spent all her time trying to avoid them. I don't think Flora even knew what she was doing or where to go or how to break the curse. I tried asking Stone, but he was too close to Flora to admit she might be out of her element.

I asked Wynn. She's doing a job and didn't ask too many questions about the quest before saying yes. Now, she feels it would be rude to suddenly 'stick her nose in the meat of the goings on'- her words. I tried to listen in on some conversations, get a feel for the rest of them. Nothing. They all seemed to believe she's a fairy princess, trapped in the body of a troll, leading us on a mission to break the curse, and that she totally knows what she's doing. But I wasn't buying it. Something was off.

"We'll head out as soon as everyone is packed up." Celairil declared, at least I think she did. Her voice is so melodic, I can never tell if she's telling, asking, demanding, or just singing a lullaby. I sat on my rock and continued to carve at the twig I had picked up after eating. By the fire, smelling the last scents of charred wood, reminded me of my mother's hearth. I'd sit and smell burning wood all day if that was an option. Because it reminded me of mom, home, and comfort.

My tent had been in my pack since before Erasto called for breakfast. I've always been an early riser, so mom says. Guess she's right. I never can seem to sleep with even a sliver of daylight in the sky. Even that first year back in Creomoxxie and she moved us to the burrow, even underground, I woke, right at the crack of dawn. I'd learned to stay in bed, or at least be extra quiet, for Mom's sake. But today? No need. I was up, tent packed, Wynn brushed and sitting with my twig, ready to whittle it a bit, all before breakfast was ready.

I had tried to get my phone out and snap a few pictures of my wings. But electronics don't work in the Fairy Realm. Erasto was nice enough to inform me of that fact when I got

frustrated and started cursing. My wings
fluttered at my back as if answering my
thoughts. I tried to still them.

"You gunna pack up?" asked a singing voice
from behind me. I didn't even look up at her. I
can never tell what elves are thinking, so I try
not to look. It's unsettling. Instead, I shoved my
thumb in the direction of Wynn, packed and
ready to go. "Hmm," was all I heard as her
footsteps headed to the fire pit.

I watched as she and Erasto spoke briefly.
I'm not excited about watching everyone pack
up the last of their stuff, so I stood for a walk.
Erasto's eyes caught mine. Crap. Now I had to
offer to help him pack up the kitchen. Luckily,
he's pretty fast and almost done. I'll get some
brownie points at least. I walked over and saw
he was placing each utensil into a long strip of
cloth. He handed me the ladle and moved to
pack the pots that made our morning oats. I
stabbed my carving into the ground, next to my
knife.

"Did you really get wings in the magical
shrink?" He asked me quietly. I paused in my
utensil pocketing, considering why he would
ask, before deciding it was probably innocent
curiosity.

"Yes. Did you?" I answered. He snorted and chuckled a little. My stomach betrayed me and fluttered in time with his laughter. That was new.

"Nope. If I had gotten wings, I'd have been gone instantly." I met his eyes briefly as he was turning to place the last pot on a pile. Erasto had not once said anything about being unhappy or wanting to leave the quest. Wait.

"Be gone from the quest? Or gone from the fairy realm? Or gone from something bigger?" I asked. He whispered a bit of magic to condense the pots and pans he had stacked into a single bag and stood to look me square in the eyes. For the first time, he looked sad, his mostly pink iris shining, with tears I assume.

"Can I see them? The wings." He asked, ignoring my question. I turned my back to him and fluttered them a bit, trying to turn my head to see them too.

"Incredible," he breathed, running his finger through them. The sensation sent chills down my spine, and I wondered what his touch would feel like elsewhere.

Focus. "I can't tell completely. What do they look like?"

"Ribbons. Ya know what I like about you, Alta?"

I shrugged and shook my head. I'm actually not sure what anyone ever likes about me.

He continued, "when you ask a question, I never feel judged or pushed to answer this way or that or like you're ever asking more than you're actually asking. With you, I've come to appreciate, a conversation is always just that, an honest conversation. No hidden motives, no beating around the bush, no reason to." He flashed me the sweetest, most honest grin I've ever seen, and for another first, I wondered what our babies would look like. "I'd fly away from this quest. I'm only here because Stone is my best friend, and he feels like he owes Flora. Something is off about this and if Stone gets stuck, I'm gonna be there to help him. I wasn't about to let him run off with a fairy princess who got herself cursed and just wait to see if he ever came home-" he stopped short.

"It's ok. I'm coming around to the idea that she actually IS a fairy princess," I whispered as I walked by him to put the utensils away. He raised his eyebrows and questioned my statement. I had been pretty skeptical. I stepped right up next to him and answer his gaze, "she's just a bit too... short. And dramatic. Especially for a Troll."

He chuckled and took the roll of utensils from my hand.

"Plus. It's hard to ignore the wings. Especially now that she can fly with them."

"Thanks for the help. And the conversation. I'm sure you wanna finish your arrow." At my obvious confused look, he jerked his head toward my carving. I stepped over and yanked it from the ground. It IS an arrow, mostly. I hadn't planned it, I had just been carving absently.

I jumped and let out a little shriek as the 'mostly arrow' shot out of my hand. It whipped up into the air and Erasto was right behind me, now, staring at it.

"Thought this quest could use some direction," he whispered in my ear, sending a chill down my spine.

"A sign! Oh Giver of Dust, guide us in our next step," Flora hollered. The mostly arrow flew around, inside the ring of trees, which was much further around now that we were all fairy sized. It finally stopped, hanging in mid-air, pointing out somewhere. I didn't know where. I'd been in Embri for almost 13 of my 23 years of existence, with only a vague clue where the other realms were, definitely no clue what was in them once I got there. "Where did this…" Flora plucked the carving from the air and turned it in her fingers to examine, "mostly arrow come from?" She looked around the now gathered group for a volunteer.

"Alta carved it this morning," Erasto said. All heads whipped in my direction and he raised a finger to his lips, giving me the keep-it-quiet signal.

Okay.

"Yeah, I was just whittling to keep my hands busy. Then, after I helped Erasto pack up, it flew up into the air before I could finish carving it." I said, leaving out Erasto's contribution. Flora tossed the arrow back into the air. It spun a moment before pointing in the direction it had been before, and everyone jumped into action.

We had our heading; I guess.

5

If you had asked me a week ago how fast I thought a unicorn could run, my answer would have fallen laughably short. The arrow didn't let up; it was fast, and the unicorns kept pace. I believe my time for underestimating the magical beasts that carried us was done. Despite being fast, it still took an entire day of following the mostly arrow before we arrived. Wynn earned every bit of her rest and pampering. Even now, Boom just sent his house staff back down to the stables to massage, sing to, feed and do whatever else the unicorns might think up to indulge in.

"Bathing and feeding aren't enough," he had bellowed, "you give them a full royal fairy spectacular." Boom Silkbite is Pinky's father.

The arrow had led us to her home and Pinky's parents, Boom and Berry, fed us, as if he had known we were coming. It was almost as good as Erasto's dinners, almost. Then he gave us comfy beds to sleep in. Then they had fed us all day while Boom and Pinky outfitted each of us with our 'perfect weapon'. I was waiting for my turn in the weapons' hold of Boom's house as the full moon crested the mountains surrounding his estate. I sat beside Erasto, but not too close, and shoved my chin at his dagger.

"That your perfect weapon?"

He held it out for me to examine. "Not sure I want to be on a quest where being outfitted with a 'perfect weapon' is necessary," he mumbled, staring at the dagger in his hand. I left it there. I didn't really want to become acquainted with more weapons than I needed to.

"But, ya know? The foods pretty good," I offered.

"Pinky's mother is a master, yes."

"I wasn't talking about Berry's cooking."

His head turned from the dagger to meet my eyes, a smile playing at his lips.

"Who's next?" Boom shouted from the door that had just swung open. Erasto jerked his thumb at me and Boom waved me over. I ambled to the armory door. Sharing Erasto's opinion, I'm not excited to need a weapon at all. But Flora is convinced of the arrows direction and the meeting of Boom being clandestine, so in I walked.

The larger-than-it-looks-from-the-outside room was... hot! Sweat immediately gathered on my forehead. How does anyone work in that place? My eyes adjusted to the warm glow, and I saw it was also filled on every wall with assorted weapons. All in various stages of completion. Metal gleamed from points and blades. Wood shone with polish. The smell of water evaporating on coals, earthy and thick, hit me hard. Maybe that's what was gathering on my forehead. I wiped it away with the back of my hand. Shadows danced across the pits and grooves of wood awaiting polish. Heaps of metal piled in corners flashed and shone in the red light of the forge, like thousands of tiny dragons, blinking eyes and puffing flames. The actual flames of the forge licked into the air, mesmerizing me. I pulled my eyes from their dance and walked around staring at wood, metal, tool, weapon, fire, flame, flicker, light, and back to Boom.

"You don't need any of these," he finally said.

"Flora seems to think we do."

"You misunderstand." He winked and walked out a back door.

Do I follow him?

Via Dyri

His head peeked back around the door frame, bearing an aww-poor-girl-doesn't-know-which-way-is-up expression, and winked again. I stepped away from the glittering metal to follow him. Outside, the evening air was still cool and crisp, and Boom was sitting on a stump, leaning on a large staff. He motioned to another stump, and I sat.

"You don't need any of those weapons," he repeated. "With power such as yours, weapons are mostly unnecessary."

Power such as mine?

"I have been holding this for just such a warrior."

Warrior? I was just about to set him straight. Tell him I'm the farthest thing from a warrior a person can be, but he beat me to the talking.

"I call it the BoomStick," he said with a shy smile. "I made it in my youth. My weapons master and teacher set me on the task. He said one day I'd meet the one for whom it was intended. This evening has brought her to me."

Me? I take a breath, again planning to explain his misjudgment. But can't really think of how to say it. Or maybe I just didn't want to. He seemed so sure.

The questions must have been plain on my face because he answered them, simply and easily.

"Yes, you," and handed me the staff.

I twirled it in my fingers and watched the knobby pattern swirl up and down. Running my hand up to the top, I noticed a rough ball shape. I stood to see it better. "It hides many secrets," he answered my contemplation. I started collecting my thoughts so my questions didn't betray my utter ignorance at handling weapons. But I was unable to ask them because a tremendous clatter came from the armory and someone burst through the back door. She looked like an elf, but I didn't recognize her.

"Alta! Boom! Come quick. The unicorns are under attack." Boom and I hurried back through the armory, across the field of their yard, around the outside of their house, across the front field, and down to the stables. The unicorns huddled under the awning of the barn, ducking and dodging as a band of five fairies were trying to hurl things at them. Rocks? But the projectiles that missed unicorns, which was most of them, shattered when they hit the wall. No. Not shattered. Crumbled like dirt clumps. Cel, Pinky, and Stone tried to throw up shields to protect the unicorns or to stop the projectiles before they got too far. It was a cacophony of splats, whooshes, grunts, and yells.

"Why don't they use their magic?" I ask Celairil as I approach. She threw me an annoyed look.

"Unicorns have no magic in the fairy realm," she answered curtly. My wings fluttered into action, and the shock on Boom's face as he jumped back, made me smile. I have a few surprises yet. I flew, somewhat clumsily, I'll admit, toward the attacking fairies, BoomStick still in my hand. One of them, a pale fairy with muddy brown curls, was shouting at Flora while the others tried to land a hit. They didn't see me coming. I swung BoomStick over my head like a batter from my father's realm. I made contact with a belly, sending one of them hurdling into his friends and taking out the entire line of them, like dominos. The fairy yelling at Flora halted, mid-word, as his friends flew past him. He looked from where his friends landed, our crew already closing in on them, to me. I tried to hover as still as I could and, taking a page from Floras book of dramatics, I swung BoomStick around my head.

"This is my BoomStick!" I hollered right at him. Somewhere off behind me, I heard a bark of laughter from Boom.

The Muddy Curls fairy seemed to consider for a moment before backing away from her. "Flora! This is not the end." He flew to his friends or crew or whatever, and they all flew away together, moaning and fussing as they went.

"Brilliant!" Flora yelled at me from the ground. "I guess Boom gave you the perfect weapon, too!"

"What was that!" I screamed at her. "Who was that?" I continued to scream. Pinky flew up next to me and took my arm. She led me back to the ground, more gentle than I would have expected a weapons master to be capable of, but more in line with what I had expected from 'Pinky the Fairy'. I landed and stomped my way directly to Flora. Stone stepped in front of me at the last second. I was about to yell at him too, when Wynn's gruff voice was in my brain.

"Don't take it out on Stone," she advised me. I considered a moment and she added. *"He's protecting her. That's his job."*

"And what about us? Who's protecting us?" I scream at her.

"What?" Stone asked, obviously confused.

"Wynn, she's defending you guys and telling me to be nice."

"Your unicorn speaks to you?" He asked me with obvious shock and awe on his face. Behind him Flora was looking from me to Wynn, shock, plain as Stones.

"Is this not normal either?" I ask, exasperated and tired of shocking people with my ignorance.

I look to Pinky, pleading. If anyone can help here, it's her. She has obviously been with Blesk forever.

"Pinky, come on." I motion for her to join the conversation. She shrugged. "What?! You and Blesk are so in sync. I figured it was cause you had been together for a while and sort of bonded." I looked at her, pleading. Only a shake of her head answered. I tossed my hands in the air, done with all of it.

"I've met unicorns before. Maybe that helps me interact better? But only one has ever talked to me, when I was a fairling. She told me the way home when I had gotten lost." Pinky's face was sad but also full of fondness, like she was remembering a dream.

"I've been talking to Wynn this entire quest. How has no one noticed?"

"We noticed," Stone started, obviously not wanting to finish the thought.

"We assumed you were talking to yourself," Cel finished for him. Celairil. Ever the realist and never afraid to just say it.

Great. I had the loser label all along.

"See, I knew you would accomplish it," Wynn laughed.

6

A buzzing sound caught my attention, and I realized everyone was hearing it. They were all looking in the direction it seemed to come from. Then I saw it. A horde of bees, horde? Fell? Swarm! A swarm, as big as we were. Well, I guess we were as small as them after the magical shrink. Either way, a bee big enough to carry me off hovered above Flora and his swarm hovered slightly behind him. Flora listened intently for several minutes.

"Right. Erlea needs me. I have to go," Flora said finally. Stone was staring at me. Expectantly. I considered, briefly, arguing just 'cause he expected me to. But really, it was too much effort, and I was pretty tired from the flying. Instead, I concentrated on folding in my wings and swirled BoomStick a few times. I wanted Flora to know I could match her drama if I needed to. As I headed back to the house, stopping just past her and looking back, I thumped BoomStick on the ground. I wanted to make sure I had her attention.

"Don't think this means I'm forgetting any of this." I thrust my hand around in the air. "Eventually, you'll have to answer my questions. Especially if your quest keeps putting us in danger. "

Erasto was waiting for me, Wynn coming up to his side.

"That was dramatic," he said. I ignored him and walked straight to her.

"Why didn't you tell me that us talking wasn't normal?" Wynn raised her eyes to meet mine. She stared at me, into me.

What was it with everyone looking into my soul?

"I imagine there will be many things I may neglect to tell you. Though not because I want to keep them, mostly." I could feel how amused she was with herself for that disclaimer. *"But more because I didn't realize that you don't know. Your ignorance seemed to be contempt. But now I see you actually were just stupid."* With that, she laughed. Well, I guessed it was a laugh. It was closer to listening to Celairil talk. Like

music I should know, but don't. Sweet, like a visit home after so long away.

How can her voice be so different from her laugh?

The group was already unicorned up, so I hopped up and Wynn fell in line. Flora said 'goodbyes' and 'thank you's' to Boom and we rode off, following the bees. We followed them through a wide glen for some time and the light of the full moon shimmered down, making the grasses look as if they were metallic. The breeze making them dance was the creepy part, though. They looked alive. I leaned forward to Wynn's ear.

"Is the grass alive?" I felt her laughing. I gave her a little kick. "A simple 'no' would be fine."

"And you don't need to speak out loud. Or kick me."

"Sorry. For the kick. I'm not sure I can think at you… sentences I never thought I'd say."

"You'll get the hang of it."

The line stopped in front of me and before I could ask Erasto where we were; I caught a glimmer of someone on the empty unicorn. Well, not empty anymore. Wynn walked past Erasto and stopped me right next to her. It's the elf that called Boom and me from his armory.

She sat a head over me, but I got the feeling that
was because her unicorn was more of a llama.
She wasn't as dark-skinned as Cel and her Anda
was green. But the patterns her Anda made over
her arms and face echoed Cel's in a familial way.
Her short, brown hair was almost boyish with
long green strands hanging in front of and
behind her ears.

"I'm Alta," I said, looking right at her.

"I know," she said, offering no more.

"We haven't met."

"We did. You just didn't believe I was there.
That doesn't mean it never happened."

*Touché. Great, another elf who doesn't like
me. I'm really wracking them up on this quest.*

She shoved her hand out awkwardly and I
realized she was trying to offer a shake. I
grabbed her hand and shook it.

"Hemlock Iceglitter. You can call me Lock.
And yes, I'm only seen in the light of the full
moon. It's an old family trait I inherited from my
mom's side. Somewhere there was a human who
had the power to be invisible. It changed in our
Elven blood to this," she gestured to the
moonlight.

"That might be the most any elf has ever said
to me at once… maybe all put together," I said
without thinking. She laughed, and my heart

constricted. The sound of her laughter was so beautiful that I was instantly filled with love, my heart actually ached, and my breath caught.

"Don't encounter many elves where you're from?" she asked through her laughter. I paused, trying to regain my breath.

"Actually, I encounter them pretty regularly. They just don't like me much, I guess." I moved my hair away and showed her my ear. Where I know the slight point of it told her what I meant. Her eyes widened but she said nothing.

"The hive!" Flora shouted from the front of the line. "Just needs my magical charms to protect it from the moon's light. Stay here. I'll only be a minute. Then we can move on."

I concentrated on Wynn. Not wanting to say my question out loud in front of the first elf to not completely shun me. I feel her gruff mind and then I hear her slightly softer voice.

"What?"

"Protection from the moon's light?" I asked in my mind, thinking of Lock 'cause the moon affects her too.

"Stop thinking about Lock. It clouds your question," she snapped. I tried again, focusing on Flora's words and the bees buzzing around the hive.

"Moonlight in the fairy realm is dangerous to those from the realm of beasts."

"Why don't they go back to their own realm? Are they prisoners?"

"Human. We may have to limit questions asked in one day." Her sigh blew through my mind and made me giggle. Then her belly extended and her lips fluttered as she let her mental sigh escape her physical body. *"The bees and the fairies are symbiotic. Well, sort of. The bees agreed to live here, and pollinate and it's the Princesses job to protect the hive from the moon."*

"Why don't the fairies pollinate for themselves?"

The bees suddenly swarmed out of the hive and up into the air. Wynn tensed under me. Lock pulled a weapon from the folds of her bags. Erasto, two unicorns up, had drawn his dagger. I guess swarming in the moonlight is not part of the expected process.

Flora jumped out the top of the hive. Her hands dripping and some weird glow floating away from her body.

"This damn Troll body!" She screamed. "No offense!" She quickly called to Stone, who was already climbing the tree to her aid. The glow that seemed to be leaving Flora was actually pulling her up. "The troll body is interfering

45

with the fairy magic!" She screamed as it lifted her troll body farther into the air. The swarm of bees was buzzing louder, and she was screaming back at them. "I know! I know! Quit buzzing! I'm working on it." Stone, reaching up, grabbed her leg and pulled her down out of the last wisps of magic. Lock and Celairil both had made it up the tree, to give their magical assist, I assume. Wynn turned, and I saw the swarm hovering above the hive. Then a loud POP and the bee closest to me suddenly had a giant wing.

Is this how fairy moonlight affects beasts? They expand? Then what? Explode? Why aren't the unicorns affected?

The bee hung in the air a moment longer, like Coyote after chasing Roadrunner off a cliff, then flopped to the ground. Unable to fly with one gigantic wing, obviously.

Pop. Pop! A few more bees gained giant appendages and fell to the ground.

"Hey, how come the unicorns aren't... effected?"

"We're not affected because we went through the magical shrink. These bees did not. They flew here and made homes but didn't shrink. They're the same size as in the realm of Beasts." Wynn shouts at me as bees are popping all around us. POP! POP! POP!

46

Bees all over are flip flopping in the grass. A leg here, an eyeball there, all comically large. One even popped his antenna larger and tumbled head over heels all the way down like a swimmer winning a gold medal. Celairil and Lock had turned their attention to the swarm and were now, I realized, trying to fend off the moonlight. Wynn hopped into a trot and headed toward the bubble of darkness created by Lock's magic.

"Make us a door into the magic!" She shouted in my mind as the muffled thumps of her hooves jar my brain with each thud.

A door? The magic bubble was getting closer. How? I'd never summoned magic that big at will.

"Now!"

I raised BoomStick and swung it, arch like, over my head. Magic swirled from my gut and sort of burst from my chest in the shape we needed. Well, mostly. Lop-sided and almost too small, a mostly door shape appeared just as Wynn jumped through it. I looked behind us in time to see my magical door swirling out of existence.

"You've got to help the bees. I have no magic," Wynn says. My brain exploded with her ideas, plans, and words, all at once and I knew what to do.

Via Dyri

I jumped from Wynn's back, BoomStick in hand, and with some help from my wings, I started my way around the edge of the bubble. First, I had to secure the magic within it. So Lock and Celairil can let it go. I drag BoomStick right along the edge of the circle, while Wynn feeds me the words for the spell. *I'm doing a spell! On purpose! And it's working.*

"Focus!" Wynn growled.

Next. Another round of the perimeter. This time, pounding BoomStick into the ground every few steps to anchor the next spell. I realize half way around that I'm making a honeycomb pattern. Wynn is a smart spell caster. I wonder why unicorns have no magic here.

"Alta!" Wynn admonished in my brain. *"Focus. It's hard enough to keep the spell on track in your mind. We can't afford to have your thoughts wonder."* Right, of course, I'm not doing a spell. Wynn is doing one through me.

Bees. BoomStick pound. Move. Pound. Hive. Protect. Bend. Bend? Why are we bending?

"We aren't. The light is. Focus!"

Sorry. Light. Moon. Bend. BoomStick, pound. Move, pound.

For what felt like hours, I focused on my task. Moving and pounding and trying to let Wynn send her words through my magic. It made my magic feel different. When I used my own magic back home, I could feel it flow from my gut. Mom called it chakras. She learned about it in the fictional realm. But Wynn's magic comes from a weird place in my brain, swirls around and then leaves through my hands. Like a stream of snow run off winding through the trees. It has a cold bite at first, but when she is done, I feel a warm release, and everywhere her magic has been is suddenly burning. Only briefly, it faded and now we were sitting inside the magic bubble, watching as the bees popped back into proportion.

Flora and the rest of the crew were gathered outside, waiting. Wynn's spell had pulled all the ill-fated bees in and wouldn't release the bubble until all the bees were back to normal. So we waited. The smell of honey was suddenly strong, and I looked to the hive, also within my dome of protection. It smelled sweet and a little- I can't place that undertone- sea salt? Probably just left over in my nose from our cliff side ocean adventure. My mind turned to Wynn and I wonder again about the unicorn's magic.

"Every creature has weakness." Wynn answered my wonder. *"Ours is that our magic is dormant until our horn is longer than a grasshopper's jump. Or a Falcons talon, depending on which mythology you subscribe to.*

*Here in the fairy realm, after the magical shrink,
our horns are no longer long enough."*

"Hmm. I expected something more, epic."

"Not everything is, Alta."

POP.

Flora ran into the circle, arms outstretched,
and I braced for the impact. But she passed us
completely and headed straight to the bees.
Fussing over them and ushering them all back
into the hive. Am I disappointed that she passed
me by? No. Of course not. I don't even care.

Wynn grunted and stomped a little. I took it
to mean, 'of course you don't care about Flora's
praise. She's not your friend. Just your boss.'

"Alta. That was impressive magic," Lock
said, clapping me on the shoulder like we were
old friends.

"Alta. I did not know you could do such
things," Celairil added.

"It was all Wynn," I patted her neck.

"It was more you than you think," Wynn
said. I ignore her, thankful no one else could
hear her.

7

Boom confirmed Keenat's prophecy, that she was the key. Have you thought about asking Alta?" Stone suggested to Flora.

"Asking Alta, what?" Erasto repeated just loud enough to make sure I heard. Wynn and I were behind them, but sound-carried-on-the-wind was our biggest friend on this leg of the trip. We had learned that Flora was counting on Stone to get to the fictional realm. We had also learned that Stone was not sure he could get back there. He'd only been once before, a long time ago and- Flora waved off his worries, claiming he was being humble and she knew he could do it.

Stone looked back at Erasto, then at me, considering how much we might have heard.

"Asking her to assist us in jumping realms when we get to the fictional barrier," Stone finally said, badly attempting nonchalance.

"What makes you think I'd know how to jump the barrier?" I asked. Stone stared at me.

"You obviously did it at least once, to get here," Flora answered for him. "How'd you do it?" She asked with that undeniable air of entitlement. Like my life, my past, was totally hers to ask about.

"I didn't. My mom did," I offered no more. My time in the fictional realm was not common knowledge. Without ever explicitly saying so, Mom had impressed upon me, those years were like a secret, just for us. I had never willing told anyone those years existed, let alone any details from them.

"You honestly don't remember a thing?" Flora asked, a frightening frown creeping across her gaping troll mouth.

I considered lying. But I'm not fantastic at it and didn't really enjoy doing it. "I remember... light. Like a burst. But that's all." I could tell by Floras body droop, it wasn't the information she was hoping for. "Sorry," I added. Watching the troll be so disappointed made me realize that if Flora had been in fairy princess form, disappointing her would have been near impossible. I was sure I would have flown right to my mother and demanded answers if I hadn't been looking at the troll version instead. I said a small thanks to the suns that the troll body gave me the freedom to not care as much. This wasn't my problem. I was a hired hand, not a savior, and definitely not a key.

A drop of something hit my hand. I jerked my gaze around before another hit my head. I shot my gaze upward just in time to get drenched.

Unicorns started running, all chasing Flora. Well, following her. But she didn't seem to know where she was going at first. She ran straight, the way we had been walking, for a while, but then doubled back, like she was searching. By the time we found cover, it didn't matter. No one was dry, and the rain had stopped.

"That storm was not normal. It was magical," Wynn said as she stomped the ground, signaling me to get off. I hopped down in a single leap, BoomStick swirling around as I did, and headed straight for Flora. Wiping the wet animal smell from my hands onto my... wet pants- crap.

"Magical storms? Gangs attacking the unicorns? Flora! What is going on?" My voice was close to screaming. I knew I should calm down, but I didn't want to. I was miserably soaked, and I wanted answers. We all deserved answers. And Wynns' grump at being wet and cold and too small to use magic was seeping into my thoughts, into my feelings and my words.

"Alta." Wynn stopped me. *"Some of your anger is coming from me. Calm down and let my emotions go. They are clouding your words."*

"Damn it! Wynn. Maybe I want them to cloud me. Flora is endangering us AND you. All of you!" I thrust my hand around the group of unicorns. "They can't defend themselves here, Flora. What is going on? Who was the gang? Who was that fairy yelling at you? And why? Of all places! Do we need to go to the fictional realm?" I stopped only to breathe and found that the wet earth smell in Volarmaa differed from what I was used to. It was sweeter, like candy had melted in the rain. And it was more calming than I'd have expected. Everyone had gathered now. Watching to see what Flora would say, or do. Stone stood poised, hand on the Boom weapon at his hip, just waiting for the order to take me down.

CRACK! Lightning shot from the sky and hit a tree nearby, bursting it into flames. I rolled my eyes and mounted Wynn, who was already by my side.

"Let me guess. Magical lightning," I said to Wynn, but out loud. I was way too angry, exhausted, and frustrated to try speaking with my mind.

"Must be. The fairy realm has rain, but no lightning."

"Of course," I rallied Wynn around to face Flora. "Magical lightning. Just here, where we are, after a magical storm. Flora, I'm going to take care of this. While I'm gone, you better think long and hard about what this quest is worth to you. Cause it's getting lower and lower on my list of priorities." Wynn took the mental cue I was screaming at her and reared up before turning in the tree's direction and trotting off. No one followed. I was glad. I'd likely have screamed at all of them.

Wynn approached the flames as close as she dared. I hopped down, BoomStick in hand, and walked one way around while Wynn walked the other way and we met on the other side. This time, thinking of my lessons at camp before we left the fictional realm, fire needs oxygen. Also, thinking about Toto and Dorothy, I swung BoomStick and with Wynn feeding me words again; I created a cyclone to suck the air out of the flame. The cyclone had to grow pretty big to get the fire to extinguish. By the time it was out, I felt several crew mates had joined the magic with hands on my shoulders, supplying me with more time. I drooped with exhaustion and BoomStick fell to the ground.

Cel picked it up and came to Wynn's right side. She chanted while holding BoomStick next to the riding blanket. It affixed to the blanket.

"Hop on, I want to make sure it's in the right spot," Cel said.

I mounted and Cel chanted a bit more, sliding the top of BoomStick right under my knee as I sat.

"This is temporary. You'll have to get a proper holster, eventually. But it should hold until the quest is over. At least."

"Cel-" my words caught in my throat.

"You don't need to spell anything, just place it back under your knee and the blanket will grab it," the corner of Cels mouth turned up so slightly I thought maybe I imagined it.

Wynn turned to thank them for the magical assist and they all disappeared.

8

ctually, I quickly realized, we had been the ones to go. Pulled backwards into a swirl of water. Like when the waves would catch me and pull me under, over and over again. Me and Wynn. At least Wynn was still with me. I could feel her echoing my thoughts, thankful she was with me. The focus on our thoughts brought us out of the crashing waves of movement.

"I hate transport by pixie dust," Wynn groaned.

But I just laid there for a minute, still feeling like I was struggling under water, breaths coming hard and shallow. Am I in shock?

"Probably. No telling what pixie dust will do to you. Part, fairy. But also elf and human... fictional human, to boot? No telling."

"Pixie dust?" I finally choked out.

"It really is the best way to get someone here fast." It wasn't Wynn's voice. I snapped up in a single jump and regretted it immediately. Wynn was already at my side, supporting me as I swayed. Hopefully our captor wouldn't notice my reaction to pixie dust travel. A tree shadow cast by the moon behind us obscured him. Which meant that we, too, were in shadow. Thankful, again.

"Who are you?" I asked in my most annoyed voice. Wynn snapped after an invisible insect, as if she couldn't care less what his answer was. I smiled, knowing he couldn't see our faces.

"Flora didn't tell you who I am?" He wasn't being smug. He was- pouting? I stepped forward, Wynn not leaving my side. He said nothing. So we took another careful, quiet step. Another. Another. But Wynn's foot broke a twig, snapping him out of his contemplation.

"Should she have?" I asked, lathering on the insulting tone.

"Yes!" He shouted. "She should have. I'm the one who cursed her!"

"Oh, that. When I asked who had cursed her, she said it wasn't important. I actually assumed she had done it to herself, accidentally." Wynn's amusement ran through my brain. I took another step, alone, running my hand along her neck as if moving to check on the beast's wellbeing. BoomStick was on the other side. It would take some creativity to get it in hand without giving away its existence.

"Done it to herself!" He chuckled. "You must not think too much of her either," he said, looking me right in the eyes. How had he closed the distance so quickly and quietly? Wynn echoed the concern and assured me she wouldn't take her eyes off him again.

"I never think too much of anyone. It's a personal policy." I tried to speak calmly, not lifting my eyes from his gaze. As long as Wynn was calm, I wasn't going to be the one who broke.

"Indeed," he answered, returning my gaze. His eyes were a murky brown. Like when they had dredged the lake, looking for Nessi. "Alta Garrison, I have a proposal for you."

"How did he know your name?" Wynn asked. I shrugged, not eager to give away that she and I were communicating.

"Who are you, again?" Was all I could think to say without betraying my curiosity or my worry.

"So sorry. Prince Field Moonweb, at your service." He stepped back and bowed.

"At our service? Seems more like 'at our captor' from here," I said.

"Ah, yes, that. I can truly say I'm sorry. It was not my intention to capture you. Only to address you privately, so as to make my offer."

"An offer? Wait-" I halted with recognition. "You were the one yelling at Flora while unicorns were being attacked. What makes you think I'd be interested in anything you offer?" I asked him, still using a Wynn-check as an excuse to move myself around her head to the other side.

"I'll not bore you with my reasons for acting the way I did, do, or will. Some things are more of a family affair. I'm sure you understand." He indicated me specifically and raised an eyebrow. This guy was creepy, and the sooner we got back to the crew, the sooner we could be done with this damned quest. When I offered no response, he continued.

"I need my sister to remain a troll as long as possible. If she makes it to the fictional realm, well, I won't get more than a few more days. So I'm asking you, Alta, to keep her from it. In whatever way you see fit, delay them, deny outright to help jump the barrier. I don't really care. Just keep her from the fictional realm until the half moon."

"No," I said flatly as I slid my foot backwards toward BoomStick. Field pouted and stomped his foot.

"Give me one good reason, why not," he whined.

"One!" I started, throwing my hands in the air to mask moving into position, "we have no reason to betray Flora. No reason to trust you. No reason to listen to anything you say."

"That was like three things," Wynn whispered. I jabbed my elbow into the unicorn's shoulder, placing my hand to rest on my weapon.

"I thought you might need a little convincing. So I have something to offer in return." He sang it a little, and it took all my will power to be still and not punch his smug little face.

"Okaaay. Would you like to know what I'm offering?" He asked.

Enjoying the awkward moment I'd created for the spoiled Prince, I stood there, hand on weapon, continuing my silence. At Wynn's suggestion, I chose my words carefully.

"No, not really. Can we go now?" Wynn and I both thrummed inwardly as the look of shock spread across his face. He recovered quickly though and started twirling a lock of greasy brown hair between two fingers.

"Too bad, really. Cause it's some pretty great info about your grandmother."

My heart skipped a beat, and the night seemed unnaturally quiet. How could a fairy prince possibly know anything about my family when I didn't know it myself? The daughter of an orphan doesn't really get to learn about her heritage. I had made peace with that long ago. Wynn pushed my heart a little with her own emotions and called my bluff. Ok. 'Peace' isn't exactly how I'd describe it.

"I'll listen, Field. But I'm not promising to help, yet. What do you know?"

"I can tell you who your grandmother is." He said it slowly and carefully, chewing on each word before spitting it out at my face.

"How could you possibly know that?"

"Let's just say my fairy grandmother is quite resourceful." Wynns laughing filled my brain and I couldn't help the snicker that escaped my mouth..

"Fairies have fairy godmothers?" I ask through Wynns laughter echoing in my mind.

"Fairy GRANDmothers," he corrected, "What do you say, Alta? Keep Flora from the fictional realm and I'll tell you what you've been wondering your entire life."

9

Flora threw her arms around me the moment we materialized in their circle. The stench made me gag, the long black hairs tickled my neck and the thick layer of blubber that was her arms was almost choking me. I patted her troll arms, attempting to comfort her. She took the hint and let go, then tried to hug Wynn but was met with a growl, grunt and a bit of bucking that gave Flora the unmistakable signal to back off. So she came back to me. With Wynn's laughter in my head, I smiled, which Flora misunderstood.

"I'm just so glad you're back. I was SO worried. We were just working on a rescue plan."

"An admittedly difficult one, as we did not know where you had gone." Cel picked up for Flora, who was busy hugging more. "Where did you go? By the way." Cel eyed us suspiciously, and I shrugged it off.

"We were kidnapped," I paused, for dramatic effect, "by your brother."

The entire circle froze. I could hear each of them breathing in the silence.

"Alta! How did you escape?" Flora exclaimed. I threw my thoughts at Wynn. We hadn't considered telling them we had escaped. Wynn dismissed it. Making up a lie like that on the spot would cause more problems than we already had.

"We didn't," I answered simply. Flora looked around nervously, as if she expected an attack. "He offered us money to lead you astray." Flora's face was more nervous. "We said no, obviously," I finished. Flora sighed and grabbed me again.

"And he just let you go?" Cel wasn't buying it.

"Before I'd even listen to him, I made him swear that no matter how the conversation ended, he had to return us here."

"He honored that promise?" Cel asked.

"Yeah, I have to be honest. He's never honored a promise," Flora interjected.

"I invoked The Winged Promise." A small gasp escaped every mouth in the circle. I ignored it. I had expected it. "This isn't my first encounter with fairies. And now?" I fluttered my own wings about, "I have leverage."

Flora's smile beamed with pride. She leaned over to Stone and whispered something to him. I couldn't hear it. The laughs of relief from the rest of the crew were drowning it out. Stone headed to his pack and started prepping to pitch his tent. Erasto was already heating water for dinner and Pinky was shaking out Blesk's blankets, probably for a pre-dinner ride.

Celairil sat on the edge of the circle, thumbing the pages of her notebook, watching me with an expression of nothingness. I wish there was an elf expression app. I pulled my phone from my pocket and tried to look one up. Dead. The fairy realm had no technologies, Erasto told me. But I had honestly, stupidly, expected my phone to work. Or I'd just gotten so used to having it available. I'd have to suggest the app to the fairies who worked at The Magic Box when I got home. An app to track Elf facial expressions? That would be a big seller if it didn't already exist.

My mind wandered to thoughts of home. My mother sitting by her hearth. The one she'd built into the wall of our house with her own two hands. That hearth was why all conversations of moving back to the fictional realm were shut down. I had always thought her attachment to it had been unrealistic. I'd even have been happy with a move to another town in Embri. One by the ocean or by the Briass river. I'd have to look into it when I got back. Maybe that's what I needed to do. Move out on my own. Was it time? It had only been a week since leaving the human realm. It felt like forever ago. Could I even go back? I had full on wings now. CoffeeMoxxie had a reputation for hiring unusual people, but wings? On a human? Yeah, a move might be in order after all.

Celairil's face shot up, pulling me out of my thoughts, then we heard Floras scream. It bellowed in my ear like a mountain avalanche. Cel and Pinky instantly headed to her side as she bumbled through her screams and tears. Wynn ran by me and I followed her. She screeched to a halt by Stone's tent, looking around for the commotion.

"There!" I hollered. Cel and Pinky were trying to help Flora to her feet. Stone lay writhing on the ground. Erasto had arrived from his fire tending and shoved me out of the way, giving me a knowing eye as I stepped back. He had feared his friend would be hurt on this quest. My heart sank for him as he looked over Stone.

"Poisoned," Erasto said flatly.

"Poisoned? How?" I asked, moving to Stone's side.

"Field! Isn't it obvious?" Flora threw her hands in the air.

I fumed. Wynn echoed my frustration. I had agreed to Field's terms. I would foil their attempts to get into the fictional realm. So why was he still using other methods? "Can you cure him?" I watched Cel and Lock moving around him.

"If we can decipher the poison's origin," she spat out between spells. "All I can tell so far is that it's fairy made." I turned and stormed off toward Wynn. She met me halfway and lowered slightly to allow me to mount quickly.

"Alta! Where are you going?" Flora shouted from Stone's side.

"We'll be right back." Wynn took off in a fury out of their circle. Once out of sight, she stopped and waited. I took a pouch from my pocket and sprinkled us with pixie dust Field had given in case we needed to contact him again. Standing in front of Field now, I didn't bother with anything close to niceties.

"What the hell, Field?!" I was already off Wynn's back and in his face. He raised a hand to hold off the guards, now moving to protect him from the sudden threat.

"I don't know. What 'hell' have you encountered?" Field asked, obviously proud of his wordplay.

"I agreed to your deal. Why poison Stone?"

He burst into laughter. "Poison? Stone?" He shoved the words out of his thin lips between gasps of laughter. "I had nothing to do with that. I've got you, Alta. Why would I waste my time, or my poison for that matter?"

"The creep makes a point," Wynn chimed in. *"Maybe it wasn't him."*

"Then why are you laughing so hard?"

"Someone else is trying to thwart Floras Quest? How lucky for me! If you fail, Alta, this mystery player might do it for us." His laughter was big and conceited. I rolled my eyes trying to paint the entire scene, thick, with my annoyance, and Wynn scuffed her feet, signaling it was time to go. I said nothing else to Field, just mounted and pixie dusted us again.

Wynn was right. It really was a sucky way to travel.

10

When we popped back into the woods near the crew, Stone's screams cut through all the woodland sounds.

Some bodyguard. I thought to myself, except apparently not to myself cause Wynn's gruff voice came hard and fast.

"You have no clue what kind of poison he fights, or how it affects his breed, especially considering his distant human heritage." I blushed. I didn't actually think less of Stone for screaming. It was a sort of knee jerk reaction. I didn't even realize I was thinking it until Wynn spoke.

"What now? It wasn't Field."

"Maybe the elves figured the poison out." Wynn said, but I could feel the skepticism under

her words. The benefit of mind talking, I guess. Wynn was already headed to the crew. Rustling leaves and scratching branches pulled my attention, and I sat back for a moment, taking in the beauty of where we were. I had missed much of the fairy realm, what with running all day to make it to Booms and now this. The forest we were in was unlike any in the human realm. Tall green trees and underbrush of varying sizes. Not that there were many forests in Embri. But here?

The colors alone had my eyes twitching from place to place, trying to capture them all. They were brown with green leaves, yes, but also tinged or tinted with other colors too. Trunks glowed like there was a colored light inside, shining through the brown bark. Blue, purple, pink, red, yellow. The leaves shook in the wind over my head and I looked up. With the moon's light gleaming down through them, the leaves seemed to glow with a rainbow of color's too. I marveled at the magical possibilities within the colors of the forest. Wynn bucked and whinnied, and I had to jump to keep from being thrown off.

"Sorry!" Wynn said quickly as she settled her feet. *"But I overheard your thoughts,"*

"Wynn! I need to have my own thoughts. Please stop listening in," I snapped at her, heart still racing from almost being bucked from my seat.

"First. I'm not 'listening in', you're talking. Two different things. Second. You may have the answer to Stone's poison. The color of the forest." Wynn said that last line triumphantly and waited. When I said nothing, she continued. *"You can magic a cure from the colors in the forest. Cel might not be able to, or even know it's possible, but you're part fairy. You can tap into it and allow it to combine with your elf magic."*

I was listening, but not being convinced or even understanding. I felt Wynn's annoyance.

"They already know you're fairy. I know you don't want them knowing you're elf, though why I can't see. So just tell them I'm helping again, which I will. But this magic is already in you, Alta. It's in you because you watch the land and you think outside the Creomoxxie box."

I groaned. She sounded like a faeble. Was she going to shove some magic shoes at me, too?

Wynn grunted, *"Faeble or not, my words are true and you know it,"* The air split with Stones screams again. *"Guess they're not getting far with that poison."* Wynn started filling my thoughts with healing spells and chants and incantations from unicorn history. I recalled my time in the fictional realm. They had hospitals where you'd go to be cured. Many had blue and white logos. The blue leaves pulsed with moonlight, making them brighter and easier to find. I reached up and plucked a few from their trees. I could have sworn I heard the trees sigh as I did. Like they were happy to help. I could only think of blue and white, but there wasn't any white in the forest. A mushroom maybe? I lowered my gaze to the grass and shrubs, but nothing brightened for me. Then I saw. Wynn's horn was glowing. Like the leaves, as if there was a light inside, a white light. Wynn saw the image through my thoughts and hummed with acceptance. She ran into the circle where the crew was knelt over Stone. Erasto's eyes were red and puffy, I could tell even in the moonlight. Lock was still visible, muttering spells with Cel. Wynn walked right between them and stopped. I hopped off and went right to Stone's side. Cel grabbed me by the arm to protest. Lock simply moved aside and jerked her head back for Cel to do the same. She looked me in the eyes, narrowed her gaze and gave my arm a threatening squeeze before following Lock to pull her out of the circle.

"Where did you go?" Flora asked quietly, not taking her eyes off Stone. He was sweating and shivering at the same time. The look on his face wasn't a look at all, it was the most painful grimace I had ever seen. And I worked in a magical coffee shop, never a place with more grimaces. Still, this was the worst I had ever seen. A shot of charisma or endorphins in his drink wasn't going to fix this face.

"Actually," came Wynns thoughtful tone, *"A magical shot might be just what our spell needs to get him on his feet, quick."*

"Erasto, can I borrow your dagger?" I asked, my hand outstretched to receive it. He stepped forward quickly and fumbled it out of its sheath. I took it, giving him as caring a look as I could. I hated to see Erasto so upset. This was just the kind of thing he had worried about. "Can you also start water to boil? I'm gonna need a cup of hot stuff in a minute." He smiled and turned toward his gear. I stepped back to Wynn, who lowered her head so I could reach her horn and I scraped.

The entire group gasped, collectively. As if they'd rehearsed it. Celairil cupped her mouth to prevent outrage. I could see it in her eyes. Flora actually cried. Trolls rarely cry, but I imagine being a fairy cursed as one gives her certain liberties. The scraping sound stiffened my back involuntarily. I could file this under things-I-learned-about-myself-on-a-quest-with-a-cursed-fairy-princess. I hate the sound of dry scraping. My spine tingled, and it almost made me have to pee. That would have sucked.

Despite her horn being inky black, glowing white dust piled into my palm on top of the

leaves I'd crushed as we had returned. I finally
had enough horn powder and stopped scraping.
Thank the suns.

"May I?" I asked Flora, not wanting to push
the princess away. She nodded and moved back
to Pinky's arms.

"I guess we're doing this with an audience,"
I said to Wynn.

*"Did you expect them all to turn around and
give you privacy after scraping my horn?"*

I ignored her. I was nervous enough. The
spell was floating around in my brain, draining
the magic from my heart and feeding the healing
power Stone would need. His hand flung into the
air and grabbed my arm.

"Nothing is worth destroying the perfection
of a unicorn's horn." His words were labored
and breathless.

"If a unicorn gives of her horn willingly,
there is no greater insult than to refuse it," I
replied, a little annoyed but also proud of my
ability to recall what little I knew about the
Realm of Beasts. Wynn settled my brain, and I
continued, "Stone. We can do this." I thought
about Wynn's comment, about my magic. "I can
do this." Stone pulled me close and let go of my
arm. He reached up and tucked my hair behind
an ear. Then, struggled through the words.

"You have your grandfather's ears. I see it now." I stopped short, all magic stalled at his words. My grandfather? I didn't even know who he was. My mother didn't know. How, under the duel suns of Creomoxxie, could Stone know? Wynn nudged me, mentally and with a nose against my elbow. Magic flowed once more and my cupped hands shook, mixing the herbs with the dust and to mask my increasing nerves.

"Erasto," I said simply. He stepped forward and handed me a mug of hot water. I dropped the powder into it and whispered as I did. The shot was the brilliant part. As I whispered over the cup, it bubbled and popped, just like the milk under a steamer at work. I smiled. My magic was powerful. I leaned over and poured it into Stone's mouth. He gurgled, gasping to gulp and breathe at the same time. The mug was empty in a matter of moments, and Flora was back by his side.

"How long…" but she didn't finish. Stone's face calmed almost immediately. His body stopped shaking and the drops of sweat popped from his skin like eggs cracked with a hammer. Flora looked at me again. "How…?"

"I'm sure Wynn fed her spells. I mean, she gave of her horn. She obviously wanted to help," Erasto stepped in. Wynn snorted and scraped the ground. Flora took it as a sign of confirmation and ran to hug the beast.

"I knew you were the most powerful unicorn I ever saw," she said, beaming with a smile from ear to ear. I thought I glimpsed Flora, the real one, the fairy, not the troll. But as fast as it came, it left. Wynn grunted, forcing Flora to let go. "I'm so glad you were here."

"We better get camp set up," Lock finally said. Wynn shook her fur as if the remains of the hug might embed themselves and cause her daily discomfort. "I suggest an entire day here, at least. Cel and I will tend to Stone and reevaluate if we can leave after another night's rest."

"No," Flora and I said together. Flora hadn't noticed me speaking and plowed on. "I'll sit with him. He's my guard. Chances are that poison was meant for me." I rolled my eyes at the dramatic turn things had just taken. Wynn punched me in the arm, mentally.

"You're doing it again. You don't know. That could be the truest thing we've heard all night," Wynn admonished.

I groaned and went to pitch my tent.

11

It was actually three entire days before Cel declared Stone was fit to travel again. I have no idea why Cel was the ultimate answer on this point. There had been plans to head out on day two, 'If he'd just get over it and ride!' Cel had screamed. Stone's refusal to travel by unicorn made the conversation moot.

"Would you like to be responsible for draining him after he almost died?" She had asked Flora in a huff when the fairy troll had suggested letting him run. No one argued, and we stayed another day. Stone was insistent that he was fine, but Flora wasn't about to risk it by going against Cel's suggestion.

I spent the three days training with Cel and Lock to learn how to shoot arrows without a bow, and trying to find a time that was appropriate to ask Stone about my grandfather.

If he could tell me, then I wouldn't have to keep that stupid deal with Field. I could call it off. Not being bound to the idiocy that was Flora's older brother motivated me to watch Stone closely for my chance. It never came. Flora stayed by his side, just as she had promised.

Now we were riding back through the fairy realm to the grove that would allow us to leave by resizing. Flora had tried to argue in favor of finishing the quest fairy sized. Not one of the crew members had supported her. If she had seen it, she would have called the mutiny what it was. Luckily, Flora doesn't seem to be in that frame of mind. Actually, there seemed to be a frame of mind all her own with Flora.

"Wynn," Stone's voice came from behind us and we twisted our heads to see him, but he stayed at her flank, head down, purposefully keeping us from seeing his face. "I'm not sure how to thank you. The dust you provided was," he paused. I was fairly certain he was wiping away tears. "Well, like I said. I'm not sure how to thank you." His shoulders shot up and his face contorted as if he was feeling sandpaper being rubbed on the inside of his skull. I knew that look. Wynn. I wanted to interrupt and ask what she was telling him. But I didn't dare.

"Correct. You don't dare." Wynn shot at me before going back to Stone. Several minutes

passed. Stone's limbs seemed to relax a bit as he got used to the sound of her voice. Finally, his grimace straightened and his eyes softened.

"Okaaay, Wynn says there is something you wish to ask me. Letting you ask it is how I can repay her kindness? You must be very special to her. She gave of her horn, for me, but now I feel it was more for you." He glanced between me and Wynn. "Well? Go ahead."

This was my chance. I could ask him about my grandfather. What he meant about having his ears. Stone could tell me the things I had been wondering all my life.

"You actually going to ask him?" Wynn's voice cut through my thoughts. I realized I had no voice, or more accurately, that I had no words. Stone's gesture on his deathbed had been so tender and kind, like we were long-lost lovers being reunited. My cheeks grew hot, and I turned away from him. I didn't even see him that way anymore, but the gesture... so intimate.

"Wynn says I told you something while I was-" he paused, clearly unable to say the word 'poisoned', "before you healed me? I don't remember saying anything. What was it? Maybe when I hear it, it will make sense."

"You said I have my grandfather's ears," I almost whispered.

"Who's your grandfather?" He asked, coming closer, obviously interested.

"That's just it. I don't know," I answered softly.

"If you don't know. How could I possibly know?" Stone questioned.

"Exactly." I said, my shoulders slumping over Wynns shoulders. Stone stiffened again, and I waited for Wynn to finish.

"She says I was remembering something when I said it and because of your link to perform the spell, she saw it and wants me to share it with you." Stone spoke softly and carefully. I perked up. A memory? Wynn hadn't mentioned it before. Three days was long enough to mention a memory.

"It wasn't my memory to tell." Wynn added to my thoughts, annoyed. *"Plus, it wasn't a full memory, just bits and feelings and colors. I figured it'd mean something to him, but it was gibberish to me."* She finished in her I-won-this-argument-and-it's-over tone.

"Can you share it? Maybe it will jog more memories you have? Or maybe it'll mean something to me?" I was grasping at straws now. I knew it. But I'd try anything to know where I came from. My father's realm isn't exactly the kind of place you brag about being from. And mom? Well, she didn't know. Being adopted at birth effectively cuts you and your kids off from their heritage.

"I can," Stone started, then looked around and moved closer to Wynn so he could almost whisper to me. "Years ago. The Elf King called on me. Never having met him, I was very nervous. I entered his throne room at the foot of the messenger, who quickly left us alone. The throne sat upon a pedestal that required stairs to reach it. Great flames burned in giant bowls on either side, though I smelled no fuel. The Elf King stood and walked down to me."

Wynn gasped.

"Is it not common for him to leave the throne? I don't understand the gasp," I interrupted.

"What gasp?" Stone asked. I pointed to Wynn, who answered the question.

"Elven Royalty have believed for eons that they are the rightful rulers of Creomoxxie. For this reason, they never leave the throne when addressing anyone not directly in their court."

"Weird," I said. Stone smiled, raising an eyebrow for permission to continue. I nodded.

"He walked right up to me and said, 'Stone, I have need of your special abilities. I must find someone and I believe they could be in ANY realm.' Of course I said I'd help and asked who I was looking for." Stone paused, sadness creeping across his face. "It was his daughter."

"Elven royalty hasn't had a daughter in five Elven generations," Wynn's words came explosively.

"That's what I thought," Stone continued, obviously having heard her words as well. "This wasn't just a daughter of the Elven royalty. This was the daughter of the Elven King and The Fairy Queen. Well, the Prince and Princess respectively, at the time they had conceived her, before each ascended the throne in their own realms. They carried her away to the human realm to be raised because the two realms are bitter enemies, each claiming the rightful rule of Creomoxxie. When the Prince became King, he immediately summoned me. I was his first order of business. His daughter was no longer with her family in the human realm. She had disappeared."

"So you went to find her." I finally put it all together. Stone nodded and seemed to wipe away tears again.

"And I failed. I jumped realms for the next three years. Until the King gave up and relieved me of my orders."

"That's why you protect Flora the way you do. You don't want to fail again," I whispered. Stone winced. "But…"

"What does this weird piece of Creomoxxie history have to do with you?" Stone asked.

"Or my grandfather," I added.

"Yes, you couldn't possibly be the daughter I was looking for. She'd be much older than you are by now. And the Elf King wears a crown of mushrooms so thick, it obscures his ears. I can't even say my statement or my memory makes you his granddaughter. Plus, he placed a Zichor spell on me. I'd have known you were her the moment I first touched you. He released me from my oath, but the spell is unbreakable, undesolvable. It remains to this day." He raised his hands, looking over them in reverence.

"The messenger?" Wynn asked, trying to help. I relayed the question.

"Helmet. Never actually saw his ears. So how could I compare the two?" Stone answered, lowering his head. "Wynn, I'm so sorry. I can see this didn't work out how you had hoped. What kind of repayment is this?" His face winced, again but he stayed mostly relaxed as Wynn spoke directly to him. He gave a short, quick nod and patted her mane. "Alta, I'm truly sorry this wasn't more help. I hope you figure it out someday." And he trotted off to join Flora at the front of the caravan. We were nearing the Circle of Elms. We'd cross the river back into

Embri and then attempt to enter the fictional realm. Then this whole thing would be over.

"What makes you think it'll be over?" Wynn asked. I thought about it.

"Cause Flora said that's where we were going."

"Just cause we're going there doesn't mean that's where it ends."

"Shit."

12

I sat astride Wynn the next day, thinking about the fictional realm not being the end of our no longer fake quest. How much farther could Flora need to go? She said we were headed there. But she actually never said that was our final destination.

Even going back through the magical shrink... or rather the magical grow, didn't take my mind off our final destination for long. Where were we actually headed? And when would we be done with this quest? Yeah, I should have asked more questions before I agreed to join.

Wynn grunted, bringing me out of my thoughts.

The entire group had stopped, and as Wynn trotted around them, we saw what had stopped

Flora. Standing in the middle of the path was a cloaked… girl. Woman? Man? Figure… holding a small object in their cupped hands.

"Who's that?" Wynn asked me.

"I don't know. I was gonna ask you," I thought back.

"You've got a lot of nerve showing up here," Flora said to the figure. I gave an audible 'ah' noise and Wynn echoed it with a little whinny. If this person was with Flora, I was happy to let her deal with them. After attacks, and bees, and storms, and magic, and wings, and no answers? Yeah, I was leaning back to enjoy whatever Flora had gotten herself into. Maybe I'd hop down and braid Wynn's tail.

"Don't you dare."

"Step aside and let us pass," Flora demanded. The figure stood motionless.

"Can't we just go around?" I asked Wynn, looking at the wide expanse of grasses, banking the river as far I could see in either direction. Wynn gave a mental shrug, and I felt it lifting my own shoulders.

"I see you found the fictional human?" The figure said. Flora and Stone both looked in my direction. "I told you she was the key to this quest. Has that not proven to be true?" Their voice gave no indication of gender. I sighed.

"How can I be fictional if I'm- Right Here?" I shouted to no one in particular. Flora and Stone returned their gaze to the figure in the path.

"Being right doesn't mean you get to join us," Flora said, with a childish pout as she crossed her arms over her chest.

The figure dropped whatever they had been holding and raised their hands. Flora winced and Stone jumped from her side to block whatever was headed her way. I marveled at his agility. But the figure just flipped the hood off his head, revealing red locks hanging shaggy down his face. His. It's a guy.

"Oh! Come on Flo! We're friends. Let it go already. I wanna help," he said with laughter and impatience.

"How do I know Field didn't send you?" Flora asked accusingly. The guy, now that I could see his face, seemed a little younger than me and rolled his eyes and chuckled as he knelt to pick up what he had dropped.

"Flora. I had no choice but to give him the ingredient he asked for. I honestly didn't know it was for… that." He gestured to Floras troll form. "You must know that. And didn't my prophesy help?" Flora looked again at me. I shifted uncomfortably in my seat.

"Yes. Alta has proven her value." She turned back to the guy, "more than you have, traitor." He dropped his head, beaten.

"Flora, he had taken Enjel captive." He offered, stroking the little object he had picked up. She gasped and hoped down from her unicorn. She rushed to him and grabbed him tight.

"I had no idea! Was he hurt?" Flora asked, holding the guy at arm's length and looking down at what he held. He raised his cupped hand for Flora to inspect.

"No. Field isn't that dumb. I'm surprised he stooped even that low. You really must have made him mad."

"Scared is more like it," Flora said with a little smile. He returned the smile knowingly, and the two shared a giggled. "Everyone! This is Keenat Gingerlight. The Fairy Prophet."

"I always thought the Fairy Prophet was a rumor cause fairies can't tell the future." I leaned to ask Lock, sitting on the 'empty' unicorn beside me.

"They can't. Keenat is a witch," she answered.

"But, Gingerlight. Isn't that like one of the biggest fairy families? They're famous even in the human realm. Don't they make cosmetics or something?"

"They abandoned him in the Elm circle as a baby. The Gingerlights took him in and raised him." My eyebrows met the sky, pulling my head up into a nod. I slowly straightened back into my seat. Things were getting pretty interesting.

"What's that thing he's holding?"

"It's my pet frog, Enjel." Keenat answered. "He's the actual prophet. I just say what he tells me." He gave a little hop as he ran to Grable. "I can't believe you actually found the unicorns."

"That was all Erasto, actually. Stone insisted he be on the crew and I haven't been sorry for it once," Flora admitted. Keenat looked over to where Flora was pointing and gave Erasto a smile.

"Impressive. For a dwarf to be in tune with the beasts."

"This reunion is great and all. But can we get on with this thing?" Cel interrupted. "The river is too wide here for the unicorns to carry us. We still have to figure a way across," she finished.

"No need," Keenat said, waving a hand at Cel. "I have a boat and now that you're not fairy sized anymore, the unicorns can fly themselves across." The earth shook as Flora jumped up and down, smacking her hands together, creating great claps of thunder each time they met.

Cel, on the other hand, eyed Keenat carefully. At least I wasn't the only one suspicious of him.

I was glad to not be on the boat. It looked like a glorified raft. I suspected Keenat made it himself. But now that Wynn was rising into the air? I was second guessing not being on the boat.

"Shut up." Wynns gruff voice rang in her head, *"your worry is distracting me from watching the raft."* She snorted, *"and hurting my feelings."*

Lock had tried to refuse getting on a raft when no one could see if she fell overboard. Cel then tried to reassure Lock that she'd feel the energy loss of that. But Lock wasn't completely convinced. She kept a firm hand around Cels' arm. Once everyone was on Keenat's boat, the unicorns took off into the air.

I hadn't even been invited into the boat. Wynn guessed it was because of our bond as beast and rider that everyone probably assumed I'd just stay on her back. I still took offense at not being asked, and was brooding until Pinky fell overboard.

13

A large rapid came from nowhere, tossed the ship and lurched Cel, who had been magicing the boat straight across the river. With her concentration broken, the spell lapsed at the exact moment that Cel was shoved into Pinky, who went right overboard.

Pinky screamed, flailing to grab hold of something. Flora gasped and shoved Stone in the arm, who moved to catch Pinky. He made contact! With her sleeve. Grasped at it wildly, only to rip the bottom half of her sleeve off. Pinky plunged into the water and immediately pulled her pack off her back. With only her head bobbing up and down as she floated away from the boat, she dug in her bag. A rope emerged from the water and she started twirling it above her head. She flung it and caught a tree branch.

Everyone cheered. As the boat neared the other
shore, every eye was on Pinky. Except for Cel
and Erasto, who were trying to dock the boat
alone. The branch snapped. I got only a picture
of a warning before Wynn tucked her feet and
dove. My head hit her rump and bounced with a
little whiplash. I struggled to hold the fur in
front of me. Wynn kept going and, with her
teeth, she grabbed the tree branch before it hit
the water. Cheers erupted from the shore as
Wynn pulled Pinky against the current.

We were now low enough to feel the spray of
the rushing rapids. My face soaking, I tried to
wipe it clear so I could see. The sound of the
water crashing over the rocks in the river was
more deafening than I thought. Or maybe that
was the blood pumping wildly in my ears. No
wonder everyone on the raft was shouting at
each other. Luckily, Wynn's voice was in my
head... not my ears-

"Alta!" Wynn shouted, *"Help. The current is
too strong."* I sat up and fed Wynn energy from
my magic. *"I'm not tired."* Wynn shouted again,
*"The current is too strong! I need you to slow
it."* How was I supposed to slow a current?
Beavers! A damn? But how? Before I could
decide, a large bulky figure jumped into the
river, grabbed the rope in its teeth and started

92

pulling Pinky across the current to the shore, the entire crew running along to meet them.

Gasping and panting, Pinky and her rescuer splayed out on the banks of the river.

"Pinky!" Came Cel's panicked voice, "Are you ok? I'm so sorry." She grabbed an arm and helped Pinky sit up.

"I'm fine Cel. Really. Alta caught the rope."

"Not Alta," I corrected. "Wynn." Pinky and Cel both looked at the unicorn in awe.

"Thank you. You bought time for," Pinky turned to see the other figure panting on the banks. Everyone had turned their attention to... a dog.

A man and woman had joined the dog, drying him off. Obviously his owners.

"His name is Obo. He's been a trained rescue dog for over 10 years. This makes his, what?" The man turned to his traveling companion, eyebrows raised in question.

"Well, about once or twice a month, at this river alone.." She trailed off in thought, trying to figure the numbers.

"More than either of us can count, I guess." The man finished, and they both chuckled as they dried off the dog.

"Obo. My life is indebted to you." Pinky hugged the beast around the neck, her knuckles clanking on the tag of his collar. The great furry beast licked her face, then stood to shake the water from his fur. His mostly white fur rattled around his body, mingling with the patches of brown and black fur. Water sprayed from him and doused everyone gathered around.

"It's getting late. Would you like to camp at our site for the evening?" The man asked as the woman settled up next to him, wrapping her arm around his and finally tucking her hand in his. Every head turned toward Flora.

"I guess Pinky could use a good night's rest," she answered.

The woman clapped her hands together and smiled. "I'm Arden and this is my husband, Rory. Lucky for you, we were already camped nearby. Obo caught wind of the commotion and we had to chase him down to see what was the matter. The Briass river can be quite treacherous. Some say it's Volormaa trying to keep the humans out."

"Others say it's Embri trying to keep the Fairies out," Rory shrugged. Arden led us off along the shoreline, around a bend in the path to a small campsite.

Everyone went to working on their tents. I tried to magic my tent up and was more successful than I expected. I took my newfound confidence and went to talk with Erasto. Passing

Pinky on the way, I stopped to lend a hand. No one was helping her. She had almost drowned and not one person was offering her assistance.

"Pinky? Can I help you with that pole?" I dodged the pole as Pinky swung it toward me, but I caught it on the down thrust and Pinky stopped. We locked eyes and I could see the red in Pinky's, even in the warm light of the setting suns. I put my end of the pole down and walked toward the fairy. It must be hard to have magic in your own realm, but be stuck here, larger than you should be, your magic not working properly, and then almost drowning? I grabbed Pinky's shoulders and pulled her close, placing my arms around her body.

What do you know? I can comfort someone.

"It must have been so scary. It scared me just watching from Wynn's back. I can't imagine being in that water-" my lame attempt at consolation. Pinky drooped and started sobbing into my shoulder. Stone walked by and caught my eye. He halted his walk mid-stride and came back. That's when I saw it. The love in his eyes. I motioned for him to come closer. He stepped over the tent and came right next to me. He stood, staring at Pinky. I started turning Pinky around and leaned her toward Stone until she was leaning on him instead of me. I backed away and Stone looked at her, his eyes wide and his expression wild. I moved my arms around the air in front of me. Stone took the hint and wrapped his arms around Pinky, who sobbed louder. I started toward Erasto's tent again but stopped and magiced Pinky's tent up before moving on.

"I saw that," Arden said quietly from across the path. I shrugged and took another step. "What kind of human can magic like that?"

"The kind that's none of your business," I answered calmly and walked on, trying to keep my wings still before they gave me away.

I found Erasto tending his fire for the evening's meal and sat beside him.

"I saw you and Wynn try to help Pinky."

"No. No. Let's be clear, that was all Wynn."

"Sure," he answered, his eyes twinkling with the thought of the secret he was part of.

"I'm serious. I was just trying to not fall off. Did you see that nose dive?" I dove my hand toward the ground for emphasis. He laughed.

"It was pretty steep." He shoved a stick into the logs and moved one over. The fire popped and hissed. I thought I might never be as content as sitting by this fire with Erasto so near me. He scooted closer. I gave him a little smile. I wanted to be sure to encourage closeness where Erasto was concerned.

"It might be worth noting that the things you have done have been pretty amazing. So you can't blame me for thinking that you'd dive a unicorn into a raging river to save Pinky." I blushed, thankful the fire light was brighter... I hoped. Erasto scooted closer. "I didn't thank you for saving Stone."

Ah. That was why he was coming in close. To thank me. But there was something more. In his voice. A longing, a sadness? I followed his gaze to where Stone held Pinky in his arms.

"How long have you loved him?" I finally asked.

"Since the moment I laid eyes on him. But, well, you can see where his preferences lie, so..." Erasto let the words hang in the air between us. I was glad that he wasn't attached, but learning that I still didn't stand a chance of being with him, kinda ruined it. I sat, not knowing what else to say.

"Pretty lucky Obo came along today," he went on.

"Yeah. Wynn wanted me to slow the current! I had no idea how to do that. Obo showed up just in time."

"Like an angel. A big furry angel beast," Flora said as she stepped over a log and sat on the other side of the fire.

"Big furry angel beast…" I echoed, contemplating it with silent giggles.

"I'm telling you. This troll body messes with everything about me. Including my ability to… talk good." Erasto laughed and Flora thrust her hands into the air saying 'see', then lowered them to warm by the fire. Erasto got up and went to start his cooking pots, leaving Flora and I alone.

"I know we haven't seen eye to eye very much, but I have to ask. Can you really trust Keenat?" I asked her, not moving my gaze from her face.

"Yes. He's never lied to me. If he didn't know, then he didn't know. Plus! Field kidnaped Enjel. Can you imagine? Not having your most important and trusted friend? We probably would have done the same thing," she finished with a shrug, as if she wasn't fully convinced, but wanted to be.

"Right. The frog… that's not real," I said. Flora raised an eyebrow, and I shrugged.

"Even in a troll body, I know not to scoff at friendship. Even if it looks different from your friendships. It's no less real." Flora let her words drift across the fire, making their way to me like slow, hot pokers to my heart. I had no friends. I wondered how Flora knew that. The Fairy

Prophet? I seethed at the idea of Keenat telling my life as if it was his to share.

But the seething didn't dull the fact that I had no one. I had no Stone to my Pinky. No Enjel to my Keenat. And I'd never even have an Erasto to my Alta.

No. The seething turned to sadness, and I lost my appetite. Bed seemed a better choice.

But first, where was my flask?

14

Next morning, Arden and Rory walked us all the way to the border of the nearest town with a market. The two of them were very interested in me, spending all morning trying to ask me questions, personal questions. I spent the entire trip trying to avoid them. Wynn offered a bit of relief when she suggested we fly ahead to scout the path. It was a transparent ruse; the path was clear and everyone knew it. Arden and Rory reluctantly left us at the town's wall.

"We're not really welcome in very many human towns," was all they would say.

"But," Pinky had tried to argue, "you're human. How can you not be welcome? This is literally your realm." They had only shrugged and turned to skirt the town completely. I enjoyed watching them squirm under her questions. Not so fun when you're the one being pried for personal details. Wynn tried to interject some wise words of warning.

"Shut it," I snapped. "They were all over me and my life for the better part of a day and they can't answer one simple question? Hypocritical, if you ask me." Wynn snorted. She didn't like being shut up. Unicorns are like that. They know better than everyone and think everyone should listen to their every word. That's actually why they stopped talking to other beings. They never listened anyway. At least that's what Wynn says about it.

"I'm going to find food and stock up," Erasto said, pulling empty sacks out of Boyle's saddle bag. I always had a hard time watching Boyle for too long. His green and brown stripes reminded me of a magicians spiral spinning wheel. The kind they might through knives at. Made me dizzy.

"Good. Let's all take a few flaps to shop around and meet on the other side of the market by dinner. We'll eat before we continue on," Flora said.

"I'll go with you," Keenat stepped up next to Erasto and smiled sweetly. "I might be useful in getting things at a great price." Erasto shrugged and headed out with Keenat on his heels. Pinky and Stone walked hand in hand into the market

and no one dared ask where they'd be going. I
looked to Wynn, already headed to the other
unicorns, who were already flying up and
headed over the market. This must be my
punishment for shutting her up. The old silent
treatment. Ah well. Not the first time I'd been on
my own in Old Ashton. I suddenly felt a grip on
my arm, and seeing nothing there, I reached for
BoomStick. Crap. Wynn had my only weapon.

"Settle down," Lock said from beside me.
"Thought I'd keep you company through the
market."

"Not walking with Cel?" I asked.

"She needs her own time. We've actually
never spent this much time together at once. It's
a little exhausting." I chuckled and heard again
the lilting sounds of the elf's sweet laugh. It
filled my heart with love till my smile hurt my
mouth. We walked on.

"I'm actually from Old Ashton. This is where
I live with my mom." We walked through the
street, staying on the sidewalk to avoid cars.
There weren't a lot of cars in Old Ashton, but it
was enough that you wanted to stay off the
roads. 'Road safety and laws' weren't really a
structured thing in Creomoxxie, yet. So drivers
went where they wanted and how they wanted.

"Oh. So you'll know all the best merchants to
visit."

"Not really." Mom and I didn't get out much. We had our nooks on our side of town, and that was kind of it. Aaaaand I had just successfully killed the conversation. Next topic. "Is it weird being invisible most of the month?" I asked as we walked along. There was no answer. "I'm sorry, is that not ok to ask? I don't have much experience with elves." The laughing came again.

"You're fine Alta, my mouth was just full." I smiled, relieved. "It's actually fine. I've been this way my whole life, so it's just kind of normal for me. When I was younger, I used to play tricks on my parents. They'd look for days before I revealed I was there the whole time. I'd sneak into adult conversations and listen… I learned SO much, way before I should have."

I wanted to ask what, but didn't want to mess up the first elf friend I'd managed to make by being nosey. Speaking of my nose, I turned down another street, following the smells to some sweet fried goodness. I bought 2 cups of fried dough covered in honey and watched as pieces disappeared right from the cup.

"I actually learned to extend my magic," she continued.

"What do you mean?" This intrigued me. Any bit of magic school I could squeeze in was always top of my list.

"When I was a baby, it was only me that was invisible. My clothes and anything I touched were still visible." I nodded, making sense of it. "I realized this at about 4 and started going naked to make sure I went undetected. But then, when I was about 6, I was eavesdropping on my parents and took a little chocolate from my mother's box. The floating chocolate gave me away, and I spent the next year learning to extend my magic to what I was wearing and touching. Except during the full moon. I can't make anything invisible then. It's like my powers go completely caput for three whole days. Ah well. Better some of the time than none, right?"

"I guess."

"You guess? But you have magic too. Aren't you glad that you have it, even if you can't use it all the time?"

"I didn't really get my magic till on this quest. It was pretty lame before this."

"Doubt it," Lock said. "Magic doesn't work like that. It's not something you get. It's something you're born with. All of it. Even if you don't realize it till later."

I hadn't considered this and felt stupid for it. My 'add shot' to coffee drinks is the main reason the Sisters had hired me. But I never considered that 'real' magic. Even though I called it 'magic', it was more like something I just always knew how to do. Which made sense now that Lock pointed it out. She grabbed my elbow tight and stopped us from walking.

"Do you see that?"

"See what?" I asked, eyes darting around the market for any sign of trouble.

"Erasto and Keenat." Knowing what I was looking for, I found them quickly. "You wanna be invisible?" Lock whispered in my ear. I turned my gaze away from Erasto and to the side where I knew Lock was standing. My face must have given away my question. "Yes. I can do that. Come on. Wanna?" I couldn't find my voice to agree, so I just nodded. Lock slid her grip down my arm until she was holding my hand. My gaze flicked from where I knew her face was based on her voice and down to my hand where I could feel, though not see, her warmth on my palm. "Stay connected to me. This is the best way." I nodded again. Lock pulled me around a corner so no one would see the human suddenly disappear.

I felt it in my hand first. Tingling, like when your hand falls asleep. Then warmth. The warm tingling dripped up my arm and rounded my shoulder. Yes. I know dripping usually goes down. I guess, unless it's from an invisible elf sharing her invisible magic with you. That's when I noticed I couldn't see my own hand. The tingling traveled across my shoulders and down my other arm while also moving down the rest of my body. I looked down just in time to see my legs fade away beneath me and I swooned. Lock grabbed my shoulder with her free hand and steadied me for a moment.

"Dizziness. It's normal. I fell down a LOT when I was a kid." I managed a laugh and felt better. Lock pulled her steady hand away from my shoulder and led me toward the fruit stand. As we walked, I could see a faint, watery shape leading me. Lock. I looked down and saw that I too was a watery form.

"I can sort of see us," I whispered. Lock stopped walking, and I bumped into her. She turned to look back at me.

"Tell me what you see," Lock said carefully. I described the forms, and Lock nodded. "Of course. You're part elf. I forget that cause you're so… human looking."

"How much?" Keenat asked, as if he was in shock. The merchant repeated the price and Erasto started digging in his wallet. Keenat placed a gentle hand on Erasto's and he stopped digging. "May I offer you something worth so much more than what you are asking for this bag of fruit?" Keenat offered. The merchant scoffed.

"Either you pay the price or you leave my line. Outsider." Erasto started digging again, and Keenat stopped him again. Keenat raised his hands and dropped the hood from his head. The merchant gasped.

"The Fairy Prophet," he whispered to himself.

"May I, now, offer you something worth more than you ask for these fruits?" The man nodded, his mouth agape and dumbfounded. Keenat leaned in and whispered in the man's ear. His expression relaxed and softened, then tears welled in his eyes and he cupped his mouth. Keenat moved back and replaced the hood on his head. The merchant stared at Keenat for a moment, then took the bag. I jerked to intervene, ready to defend the deal Keenat made. The merchant was obviously trying to back out on it. Lock held me tight.

"You're invisible. Don't out us."

The man turned and filled the bag till it was bursting and handed it back to Erasto with two hands, as if the fruit itself was his own precious newborn babe.

"What did Keenat tell him?" I whispered.

"His prophecy. Probably. It's kind of his specialty."

I stared at her blankly.

"Is the Embri really this ignorant of the way the realms work?" I winced at being lumped in with the ignorant humans. "Sorry. I'm not saying you are dumb. I'm just honestly curious. You seem to know little about the realms outside of your own."

"My mom didn't let us travel much. And maybe. Maybe the human realm is kind of isolated from the other realms."

"Everyone has a prophecy," Lock explained as we walked through the market. "It's kind of like a destiny... except it's translated into words and then interpreted. The trick is finding someone to translate it. Even then, it's not guaranteed that they can interpret it... or that you'll understand it when they do. Which is why they seem more rare than they are. The prophecy is quite common. Understanding it? That's the real rarity."

"Sounds like it's still worth a shot, though. Even a chance to find out what you're meant to do or be or whatever," I mused.

"Not really. Causes more confusion than clarity. Which, for most Realmians, leads to more pain than if they had just lived their lives." I was about to argue when Lock stopped me and pointed. Stone and Pinky were walking into a weapons shop. Lock gave my hand a little pull, and we jogged to the window on the side of the building. I had to suppress my glee. I had never had a friend to sneak around with. To whisper in alleys and spy on people with.

"I like this one," Pinky said, picking up a strange weapon I had never seen.

"I think if you want to say thank you by giving a weapon, it should be a practical one." Stone offered. "But what practical use does a dog have for a weapon?" Pinky laughed, and Stone joined her. The laughter of a Fairy, too big for her breed and a Troll too human to fit in his own realm, sounded like a tangle of wind chimes. You feel like it should sound nice and soothing, but it sounded like rocks clanging haphazardly against sheets of metal.

"This one?" She asked him and held up a small dagger with a fancy sheath.

Stone nodded and said, "I think Arden and Rory will love it."

"Help!" A voice from the back of the shop called. Pinky dropped the dagger onto the counter and followed Stone through the door to the back. Lock and I ran along the building, hoping there was another window. Luck!

"Hello?" Stone called, coming into the room first.

"Yes. I'm here." The voice came from outside the back door. Pinky ran to it and Stone stopped her with his arm across her path. He pushed his finger over his pursed lips. My heart dropped. Stone really was so very kind and sweet. I wallowed in my own lack of someone to stop me from running into danger.

"Hello?" The voice called again.

"Yes. We're here. How can we help?" Stone said in his most beefy voice.

"I've been mugged and I think my leg is broken," they answered.

Pinky gave Stone sad eyes as she tilted her head.

"He sounds little," she whispered. "Come on Stone. Not everything is a trap."

"Everything has the potential to be a trap. It's what has kept me alive."

"How many enemies have you made?" She teased him, then ducked under his still outstretched arm, turned to kiss his cheek, then moved to the door and pushed it open. "Stone!" She called as she exited into the alley.

Lock and I ran to the corner of the building and saw a young boy stuck under a huge wooden beam. Pinky was already trying to move it when Stone came through the door.

"Can you lift-" the boy's scream cut off Pinky's question. "Please, we'll have you out in a moment."

The boy stared past her right to Stone and raised his finger. "T-t-tr-Troll," he stammered out before going white and screaming again. Pinky knelt beside him, attempting to calm him with a hand through his hair.

"This is my friend Stone. I promise you, he will not hurt you. He can lift this beam. He's very strong."

"I know trolls are strong." The boy practically spat out, "who do you think did this?" He swept his hand over the beam and then touched his cut head gingerly. Stone grunted and lifted the end of the beam nearest him. Pinky pulled the boy just out of its path. He screamed as his leg dragged alongside him. Stone placed the beam back down and started toward the boy.

"Stay there, Troll!" He shouted. Pinky's eyes narrowed, and she turned on the boy.

"Would you like my delightful friend to lift the beam so I can drag you back under it and you can wait for the awful trolls to come back and finish the job?"

I laughed and Lock yanked me back around the corner as Stone twisted to see what the noise was. We stood, watery forms against the wall, waiting to see if Stone would come to investigate.

"Stone, can you carry him back into the shop?" Pinky asked, and we heard Stone's footsteps descending the alley a bit. The boy screamed at the action of being lifted and Lock and I, swung ourselves back around the corner to see the boy bite his lip when Pinky shot him a look. They walked back into the shop and closed the door.

I moved to head back to the window, but Lock held me in place.

"I think we should call it a day for the invisible duo and head to the other end of the market," Lock suggested. She walked us to a spot further down the alley, with no chance of being seen accidentally by our crew mates, and pulled the magic off my body. I felt it sluff off like a dried mud bath flaking away.

"I think that was the most exciting day I've ever had." I said as I shook the last flakes of invisibility off.

"But you got wings in the magical shrink."

"This was better."

Lock laughed. Had I just made an actual friend?

15

Alta!" Verian screamed from behind the counter. She dropped her mugs on the wooden countertop and called out the names for the orders as she rounded the end of the counter and headed to me. She wrapped her arms around me and squeezed. I stood, frozen. Verian had never hated me like most people did, but we had never been close enough to expect this. The petite frame of Verian finally let go and tossed her blue hair back. "Where have you been? At first, the sisters tried to say you had run off and joined the circus. We reminded them that the circus was fictional, and you were real. Then they tried to tell us you'd taken a sick day. We explained it had been more than a day. Then they tried to tell us you'd run off to join a quest to save the fairy princess from

a terrible curse. We stopped asking after that-"
she took a breath.

"Well, I kinda-"

Verian cut me off, "Oh! Let me start your
drink. Whattaya want?"

I followed her to the counter and ordered.
Verian moved to make my drink.

"There's one more drink," I stepped aside and
when Lock started ordering, Verian's eyes
widened. She looked around for where the voice
was coming from.

"Alta, that's freaking me out. How are you
doing that?"

"I'm not, my friend, Lock," I held my hand
out to the side where Lock was standing, "is an
elf. She can only be seen by the light of the full
moon… but she still likes a drink now and
then." Lock finished her order and her watery
form started rummaging in her satchel.

"I got this one. Least I can do for the fun
today," I said, stopping Lock's arm from digging
for money. Verian eyed my hand, trying to make
out the elf I claimed to be with. She raised a
finger to question further, but was interrupted.

Three figures came from a panel door in the
wall. All three stopped and stared Lock in the
eyes. It would not surprise me at all if they could

see her. Those Sisters were shiftier than anyone they ever hired. Their secrets ran deep, I'm sure.

"Alta. You've returned," the middle one said.

"No. Just passing through on our quest," I answered, moving Lock to the end of the counter to wait for our drinks.

"Be sure this elf doesn't steal anything. Or it's coming out of your check," the first said, thumbing toward Lock. I rolled my eyes, turning my back to them, and ignored the slur. Then the third gasped. I felt a tingle go down my spine and I jerked myself forward, out of their reach.

"Wings?" The third said as the middle sister stepped back through the panel door. "What a quest this must be," said the third. The middle one returned through the door and thrust a box into my arms.

"This is all your things," the middle sister said.

"We'll not have half fairies working at this shop," the first continued.

"So people can come just to gawk at the shopgirl?" The second asked.

"No," the middle answered, and they left through the panel door.

"Did you just lose your job?" Lock asked as the door clicked shut. I nodded and pulled our drinks from the end of the counter.

"Yeah, we should get you a cloak or
something. You might find more times when
covering those beauties saves you," Lock
whispered in my ear.

Cloak. Noted.

We stepped outside into the courtyard,
leaving the familiar coffee smell behind, and
found a small table. The courtyard outside
CoffeeMoxxie had a central fountain and
flowers lining the shop entrances. I was just now
noticing how nice it was to sit and enjoy the
plaza. I'd worked there for three years and never
once thought to do it. Flora walked by and we
called her over.

"Oh. Am I glad to see someone I know.
Trolls are not popular in the human realm."

"I hear the only ones here are thugs and
muggers." Lock offered, picking up her drink
and letting it stay visible. Maybe she finally got
tired of disappearing completely.

"Oh! Lock. I didn't even know you were
there."

"Did you think I was drinking two cups by
myself?" I laughed. Flora blushed, even through
her thick troll skin.

"She's just teasing," Lock amended.

The door swung open and a deep voice
greeted us, "Flora. I'm so glad you made it safe.

This place is so 'troll unfriendly'," Stone said. Pinky followed him out of CoffeeMoxxie.

"Were you guys in there this whole time?" I asked.

"Alta!" They shouted in unison, tilting their heads with expressions of pity and hugging me. Lock laughed, and I had no choice but to join her.

"I missed something," Flora said, eyeing the bunch of us.

"Nothing important," I finished. Stone walked around to sit next to Flora, and Pinky squeezed herself behind my chair to an empty one on Flora's other side.

As she rounded my chair, she leaned over and whispered, "Sorry you got fired. That stinks."

"It's alright. I wasn't sure I'd come back to work here after-" I fluttered my wings to finish my sentence.

Pinky nodded and sat, holding her hand out to Stone. Ugh. They were going to be all cutesy. He looked at her blankly before peeling coins from his pocket and giving them to her. "Told you." She mumbled, then gave half of them to me. "Only fair if I make money off you unknowingly, that I share it." I liked Pinky. Even if she was betting on my misfortune.

Via Dyri

A ruckus caught everyone's attention. A small cart was being pushed noisily along the cobblestone courtyard.

"It's Erasto," Lock said. Stone jumped up and ran to the cart to take the handle from Keenat. But before he could, it immediately stopped clanking and sailed smoothly over the cobblestones. Stone and Erasto looked to the group. I raised my hand. Pitching tents and moving carts? I could do magic in the human realm. Real magic, not just shots in a mocha.

"Wow. Erasto. How did you get so much with our little purse?" Flora asked, staring wide eyed at the mountain of food piled on the cart.

"Keenat. He was right. He's quite skilled at getting his money's worth during negotiations." Keenat lowered his head and smiled.

"Well, I didn't do it all. Without Erasto, I would have gotten a year's worth of berries."

"Yeah, and they would have gone bad in a week," Erasto countered. They laughed at some inside joke, touches lingering a bit too long on each other's arms, and I felt a brief stab in my gut. Not only did I get denied a chance with Erasto, now I had to watch him fall in love with someone I didn't fully trust. After losing my job. The cart dropped with an uneremonious thud by the table and I slid my chair out and walked away.

I perched myself on the edge of the fountain and reached down to feel the cool water. I saw Lock's watery form sit next to me. She said nothing, but I felt a hand on my shoulder. Shouts of exclamation tuned our heads. Shoppers were pointing to the sky and everyone turned to see an aircraft circling the courtyard. Lock and I jumped into action, heading for Flora. I noticed the crew assembled around her. We joined them and waited. When the craft started sky writing, everyone relaxed.

'Teresa, will you marry me?' I plopped myself back into the chair. Really?

"Oh! How exciting," Flora exclaimed. "I wonder who Teresa is," she said, glancing about the courtyard wildly.

"There," Pinky shouted, pointing to a girl in a long flowery dress, holding flowers to her nose as she watched the sky. Her short green hair flying in every direction as the wind picked up. Then she gasped, and every eye went back to the plane. The door had swung open, and a man was hanging from the edge. Then he jumped.

His parachute opened almost immediately, and the air thrust him backwards as the winds took hold. His newly proposed bride gasped again and rushed forward as passersby screamed. He settled into a nice air stream and started coasting to the ground, slowly, toward his bride. The now gathered crowd 'awed' in sweet unison. I felt sick.

Finally, the man landed expertly; I noted. The crowd erupted in cheers and applause. He dropped his gear in one fell swoop as he walked to his bride, or soon-to-be bride, knelt on one knee and produced a small box, which he offered to her. She nodded frantically, shoving her hand into his to accept the ring. The crowd cheered again, and the applause was too much. I got up to leave the courtyard.

"Alta! Don't go now!" Flora shouted over the applause. I waved her off and kept walking. "But I got us all rooms," she was pointing at the hotel across the courtyard, "Thought we deserved a night off the ground." The rest of the crew renewed their cheering, for Flora this time. "Since we're passing through. Ya know?" Flora added at my obviously annoyed look.

I skirted the large group still applauding the newly engaged couple until I got to the hotel doors. I slid inside and was momentarily relieved at the silence the shut doors provided.

"Yeah. Just now! Someone got engaged out in the courtyard." A bellhop shouted to a desk clerk.

"Wow!"

"Yeah, the guy literally dropped from a plane." The desk clerk's eyes went all dreamy, and I searched the lobby for a sign to the bar.

Mom would be upset to learn I had been here and not said hi. But there was no way I could handle her 'you need friends, Alta,' or her 'ya know? Friends can lead to more... but you kind of gotta talk to people first.'.

My mother didn't know how I was actually trying. But after this day had taken a sudden and ugly turn for my heart? No. I'd skip home, my bed, and all my mom's questions and lectures, and drown my sorrows instead.

That was adulting... top tier.

16

"N ice cloak," Flora said, slowing
Grable from the front of the caravan
to walk beside me. "I like how it can
show off your wings like that."

*Why was she trying to make
conversation? Couldn't she tell I was sulking?
And maybe hung over?*

"Alta, I just heard about your job."

I shrugged and grunted a little.

"If I had known, I would have said
something to them."

I bounced my eyebrows, helplessly, hoping
Flora would drop it.

"I mean, I feel like it's kinda my fault. With
this quest and all," she finally stopped, waiting
for me to reassure her it wasn't her fault. I said

nothing. It was, absolutely her fault. Grable finally trotted off, taking Flora with him.

"Kind of mean. Don't you think?" Wynn asked as Grable's tail swung out of sight. I shrugged again. *"Seriously. Can this Erasto thing really be that life altering? It's not like you were even close to being with him."* I wished I could just fly away… I had my wings, but I was too heavy to use them in the human realm. *"Alta, really. Erasto didn't even know you were remotely interested and now you're going to shut down just cause he's all flirty with Keenat? Kind of childish."* Wynn was goading me into speaking. I could feel it.

"I am not! I'm honestly annoyed at your behavior."

"MY behavior? Erasto's the one getting all cozy with the enemy."

Wynn smiled, satisfied. I rolled my eyes at her smug feeling in my bones as she did. Smug is way worse when you have to feel it too. I gave Wynn a small kick on the side. She returned the jab by rearing up and almost dropping me off her back end.

"Fine," I said in our minds, as Wynn came to a walk again. *"Last night, at dinner? Ugh. Then this morning? I'm suspicious they spent the night together."*

"So what? I know you're heartbroken and all." I felt Wynn roll her eyes as she spoke. *"But he's still your friend. Be happy for him to have found someone to get his mind off Stone."* Wynn encouraged. I huffed. Wynn smiled brightly, to be sure I knew she had won.

The day was bright, yellow, sunny, and perfect. I hated it. Elgar, the 'empty' unicorn, sided up to us and I felt Lock place her hand on my arm. Doing nothing more than grasping it for a moment, I calmed.

"Back home, I could count on a little rain when I felt like it."

"Is that because you can control the weather there?" Lock asked, amazement in her voice. I laughed. Out loud. Several unicorns slowed and heads turned back to check on me.

"No one controls the weather there."

"Then how can you count on it?"

"It's kind of an expression, I guess."

"I'm so excited to visit the fictional realm. Is it true they have no magic?"

I nodded a confirmation. Lock blew out a breath of air. "It really must be miserable there. No wonder your mother left. Hey. Have you thought about asking her how to jump realms?" I hadn't. She had always implied that someone else got us through the barrier. But now, with the wings and the magic. Maybe a conversation with Amethyst Garrison was in order.

I covered my ears as a blaring gong sounded in front of us. I leaned to one side, clearing my view around the line of unicorn's and saw it. The tall tower blocking the path we had been on. How had I not seen it sooner? After looking into the sky for the top, I can honestly say it's a million stories high, at least. Had I been so engrossed in conversation with Wynn and Lock that I missed a looming tower reaching into the heavens? Not that it was my job to watch for nefariously tall towers. I tried to shake it off. But the nagging feeling that I should have seen it coming was nestling in the back of my brain.

"I am Flora Moonweb, Princess of the royal court and Heir to the Fairy throne. We seek admittance to the fictional realm. Open your gates and let us pass." I leaned further. Would that kind of decree just... work?

"You're no fairy, dear." Came a scratchy voice from somewhere up the tower. A big crow sitting on a window ledge flitted and ruffled its wings so everyone could see who had spoken.

"Did you know there are penalties for claiming to be of the royal fairy court?" Came another voice from a window several stories above the crow. I looked but couldn't see who it was.

"Wait. Are you lot riding unicorns?" The crow asked in shock and began laughing so hard he tumbled over the edge and started falling. Flora gasped, starting to scramble off Grable. But the crow stuck his wings out and fluttered them a bit to slow his fall before landing on the ground in front of her. Behind him, a figure jumped out the window it had been watching from and swung on vine, brick and post, down the outside of the tower before jumping wildly and landing beside the crow. Who offered a wing, which the monkey slapped in a friendly high five.

"Ugh." Keenat rolled his eyes in disgust. "These guys."

"Unicorns," the crow said to the monkey. "When was the last time folks riding unicorns tried to get to the fictional realm?"

"Oh," the monkey answered, flipping and flopping around in excitement, "that would be…" he thought for another moment, allowing himself to jump back to the tower, climb up a bit and swing from a post. "Never! If I recall correctly."

"You DO! Monkey. You recall correctly. Never has a group riding unicorns sought admittance to the fiction realm via our tower."

"Now Crow, why do you think that is?" Monkey asked, swinging lazily from his post. I got down and walked to the front.

"Oh, Monkey my friend. It's because unicorns lose all their powers in the fictional realm, becoming plain, boring versions of themselves, forgetting everything about the Realms and never returning," he answered with a thin smile across his beak.

"Flora, the border is wide. Let's find another place to jump the realm." Stone said, trying to sound calm. "We can figure it out elsewhere," he tried to whisper.

"Yes, Alta?" Flora said sweetly. Well, as sweet as a troll can. I petted Grable on the face and ran my hand down the unicorn's neck as I walked closer to Flora's face. She leaned down. I kept my back toward the tower and its guards, raised up onto my toes and whispered to Flora.

"Wynn says it's not true. The unicorns can and will make the trip." I finished and strolled back to Wynn without another word or a glance back.

"I think we'll take our chances, Crow. Let us pass," Flora said as she rose in her seat to display all her troll fairy might.

"Oh, my dear, it's not your choice," started the Crow.

"Yeah. It's the trial that decides," Monkey added.

"Trial," Stone said flatly. "Flora, last time I was here, the trial almost killed me. Let's find another way."

"The Key," Flora said, jerking her head to the back of the crew, "and her unicorn are with us. I feel like we can't fail."

"Great, Wynn. Now what are we supposed to do? Field has information that is too valuable for me. If we help them cross the realm, he won't-" Wynn grunted to stop my rant.

"If you help. But I'm not beholden to your deal. Nor are my herd mates."

I huffed, but said nothing.

"I accept your trial, Crow," Flora was saying as she dismounted Grable. "What must I do?"

"You must answer me these questions three," Monkey said from his perch.

"What questions Monkey? I'm ready," Flora said, her chest puffed out.

"Questions?" Stone started, "My trial was a test of physical strength and-"

"Oh, dear," Crow started. "How adorable that she thinks she'd be the one to pass the trials into the fictional realm. You Trolls can't even begin to understand the questions put forth by the tower," Crow went on. Flora only stood, listening. "No, my dear fairy troll. She is the one who must weather the test." Every gaze followed Crow's outstretched wing to the back of the crew where I stood by Wynn. I looked up.

"Oh no. I don't do Trial by Crow," I looked over to the tower, "Or Monkey." And I climbed up on Wynn in what I hoped was an act of finality. Wynn, however, had other ideas and walked me right to the front and stopped in front of Crow.

"Seems your pet has other ideas." Crow started, but stopped when Wynn closed the distance instantly and had her horn at his throat.

"Pet, indeed!" Monkey shouted from the tower. Still swinging from perch to perch, he continued, "What is the center of gravity?"

"Gravity?" Flora asked in that high-pitched tone, that no regular troll could reach, that meant she was shocked and offended. "At least ask questions about real things. I've never heard that word before in my life!" She finished with a cross of her arms and her troll nose stuck high in the air.

"V," answered Stone loudly. Then he turned to Flora, "It's what the fictional realm thinks holds them to the land."

"Stone. How do you know that?" Cel's voice came from behind him.

"I spent some time in the fictional realm," he answered quietly. "A long time ago."

"Then maybe you can answer these questions." Cel and Stone turned to Crow, eyebrows raised in hope.

"As long as it's not the fairy troll," he said, tossing his hands in the air. Stone smiled and stepped forward.

"What do you have to break before you can use it?"

Stone dropped his head to consider. Cel raised her fingers to her chin. Pinky started bouncing in her seat with her hand in the air.

"Yes, my dear," Stone called without looking up.

"The Bones of Prophecy," she answered proudly.

"Well, if we were questioning the Realms, that would be a fine answer, my Pinkalicious. But they don't have those in the fictional realm," he answered, still bowed in thought. Pinky slumped herself over Blesk and patted the beast's mane. Suddenly, Stone jerked up as his body went ridged. He stood, stiffened and staring over the tower but not really looking at it. Wynn. I looked down at the unicorn I was sitting on, who just shook her mane and brayed a bit to distract Crow and Monkey.

"An egg," Stone finally said.

"An egg? But eggs get broken when they hatch. That's when you're DONE using them," Flora cried, tossing her hands in the air and almost falling off Grable.

"In the fictional realm," Stone started, but thought better of it. "Well, let's just say it's different there."

"Different how? It makes no sense. The egg hatches, the shell gets discarded, and the animal is born. How is that breaking it to use it?" Flora was almost screaming in exasperation now.

"They eat them!" I shouted. "They take the eggs before they're fertilized, crack them, cook the insides and eat it," I finished. Erasto, Cel and Lock all gave audible groans of disgust. Pinky gasped and actually started crying. Flora leaned over the side of Grable and wretched. Keenat seemed unaffected by this news. I wondered if he knew it or was really just not affected. Stone looked at me with his lips pursed and his eyebrows raised. "Sorry," and a shrug was all I could offer him.

"Ok, Monkey. Two down. One to go. Let's hear it?" Stone asked, confidence in his voice.

"Take off my skin and I won't cry. But you will," Monkey said simply.

"Take off my skin?" Flora cried. "What kind of hell are we headed to?"

"It's not a regular question, Flora," I spoke carefully. "It's a riddle." She looked at me blankly. "A question asked in a way that makes you think it's one thing, but it's actually another."

"Why can't you just ask directly?" Flora whined.

"It's a way of keeping your brain sharp."

"They sharpen brains?"

"Ugh." I regretted my explanation attempt.

"It's an expression, Flo," Keenat stepped forward. "It means they challenge their brains to keep them smart."

"Why don't they just say that?" She asked, panting. Keenat just shrugged and went back to Erasto.

"So what is it?" Flora asked no one in particular.

I knew it was an onion. But my deal with Field meant I couldn't help Flora into the fictional realm. Stone went stiff again, but not as much. Was he getting used to Wynn's voice?

"An onion," he announced triumphantly.

Crow flapped his wings wildly and Monkey stretched as he swung from pole to pole. Crow took off into the air and perched back on the top of the tower, while Monkey lumbered over to Stone.

"But only ONE may pass!" He shouted at Stone.

17

W hat?!" Flora raged. She jumped from her unicorn and lunged toward Monkey. Stone caught her and pointed. Monkey was doubled over, laughing at his own joke. Crow was snickering behind his wing, looking down from another window. Flora righted herself and glared at Monkey.

"I'm just kidding," he spat through his laughs. "You weirdos are free to pass." He stepped aside as the doors parted at the center and swung open toward us. We watched the light pour out from within and shielded our eyes from its bright rays. The light didn't wane. No one moved.

"So, what? We just walk through?" Erasto asked.

"Um, can we go back to the unicorn's plight?" Pinky asked. "I won't go if Blesk and the others can't come back."

"It'd be real helpful if other unicorns talked to their riders, Wynn." I said, as Stone went to calm Pinky's worries.

"And what about the rest of us magical beings?" Lock said from her seat on Elgar. Everyone whipped their heads to the 'empty' unicorn before remembering about Lock. "I didn't sign up to go where my magic doesn't work, especially if I'm likely to forget I even have it and that I belong in another realm."

"You didn't sign up for anything, Lock," Flora shouted. "Cel did. You just got swept up in it. You're free to stay." I wondered if Lock saw it for the bluff it was. There was something about Flora's posture that told me she was on high alert, tense.

"I go where Cel goes," Lock started. Cel looked to the space above the unicorn's back and widened her eyes. "For now, anyway. So I'll be going. I'm just voicing concern. Alta's right, no one here questions the madness and I, for one, am not walking blindly, literally!" She stuck her hands out toward the glowing doorway, but I knew it was a missed gesture, as no one could see her. "Into a world that could erase my memory of who I actually am." She paused, but

no one dared speak, as she might not be done
yet.

"Lock," I started, "I came from the fictional
realm. My mother came from there as well. If
she can remember the Realms during her time
there, I'm sure you can too."

With that, Elgar walked on. Spurred by
Lock? I assumed, but couldn't be sure. Once
Elgar was on the path, the other unicorns
followed suit. All seven unicorns, eight riders, as
Keenat was riding with Erasto, I noted, and
Stone walking beside Grable, stepped up the
seven stairs. I marveled as I looked left and right
to see the entire crew walking forward, together,
side by side, to the lighted doorway. I tried to
close my eyes to the light, but Wynn fed me a
spell to allow me to look through it instead. Was
the doorway growing? I asked myself as we got
closer. From the ground, it didn't look big
enough for us to enter side by side, but now I
was looking down the line of unicorns, to my
left and right, and we all seemed like we would
fit. It must be growing. Or at least it was bigger
than it looked, obviously.

"Or we're shrinking," Wynn offered,
"again."

"No!" I gasped, *"You think?"*

"No. I don't." Wynn answered, snickering in her mind. I thought about giving her a good kick in the ribs.

"Not unless you want to be bucked into the fictional realm by my rump," she answered my thought.

I looked around the doorway, and with the help of Wynn's spell, could see it was… plain and boring. Simple stones were stacked until they met in an arch overhead. Grey stone, grey mortar, no carvings, no art. Nothing. Where was the light coming from? As I thought the question, Floras exclamation from ahead, pulled my attention and I realized we had ended up in a straight line again. During the hallway of light? Must have been, I told myself.

Coming out of the doorway, I saw what Flora was looking at. The land we had come to was a forest. Light streamed down through the trees and into the small clearing we now occupied. Tall trees towered over us, like the tower we had just passed through. Green leaves fluttered in the wind above us. I took a deep breath, remembering the forest. Trees being green and… normal. I took another deep breath, enjoying the silence as everyone wondered at the sight.

"The sky…" Pinky started, "It's blue."

"Must be dusk then," Lock finished.

"I think it's midday," I said absentmindedly. I felt every head turned to me. I continued without looking at them, "Its always blue here." I added, "I say mid day cause the sun is up there." I pointed up, and every eye followed. "It moves across the sky as the day goes on."

"Ah-maaaazing," Erasto crooned.

"This place is actually beautiful," Keenat said. "Why would anyone leave it?" Was he coaxing me into an argument?

"Probably not. I doubt he cares enough for that," Wynn cautioned. I gave her a mental snub and went back to enjoying my deep breaths of the forest air.

But it didn't take long before it was interrupted again. This time by someone not in our group.

"Catch it! Catch it!" A man was shouting, his voice mumbled by the thick beard on his face. I know that's not how beards work, but not seeing his mouth made my brain fuzzy for a moment. He was tall and thin and his floppy brown hair flew behind his head as he ran, chasing something, shaking a stick in the air.

"Don't let him catch me." I snapped my head around to the back, where the tiny voice had come from. I saw nothing. Wynn sent me a feeling of fur twitching on her rump, and I zeroed in on where the itch was. "Don't let him

138

catch me. He only wants my magic!" The tiny voiced pleaded. I still couldn't see who, or what, was talking.

"*Magic?*" Wynn asked. "*I thought the fictional realm didn't have magic.*" I echoed the thought while still looking for,

"Ah! Wynn, it's a butterfly," I said triumphantly, proud I'd found the tiny voice amongst the grey shaggy fur of Wynn's rump. Then turned to the man now, running toward our group.

"Did any of you see a butterfly go by?" He asked, in panting, short bursts as he tried to catch his breath. Everyone looked around, shaking heads and shrugging. The man took his stick, which I now saw was actually a net, and ran on in search of his prey.

"Thank you for not giving me up," the butterfly said to me as it settled on my shoulder.

"Can you tell us how to get back?" Flora asked gruffly, as Grable trotted over. The butterfly ignored her, but I looked at Flora as she asked, and for the first time, I saw no one looked the same. The unicorns had all lost their colors and now wore plain browns, whites and blacks. Though the patterns were the same so I could mostly tell who each one was. And thankfully, through their unicorns, I could deduce who each rider was. Flora now looked fully human. She was a thin, frail looking young child. Stone standing next to her, was an older man with a white beard and shabby green pants. I looked around the entire crew and realized now. This was what Flora had actually been exclaiming at when we'd first come through the portal.

"Wait," I interrupted my own thoughts, "Go back?" I turned to Flora, and Wynn rounded on her as well. Stone stepped between us. "Why would we go back? We haven't done anything here. Isn't there a reason we came here? Something we must get? Or do?" I could feel my anger rising and Wynn tried to pull me out of it with thoughts and feelings to calm me. I jumped off and walked as close to Flora as Stone would allow. "Flora! Now is the time for answers. I want to know exactly why we're here and what the hell is going on." I sat myself on the ground in defiance. Wynn dropped her rump into a sort of sitting position, and every unicorn followed suit. Even Grable. Though he waited till he was the last one, I eyed him. With their rides down for the count, everyone else sat too. I hummed with a little satisfaction when Lock came to sit beside me.

"Way to make a stand," she whispered as she sat.

"Or a sit." Cel added as she too took a place near me. "Sit, stand or ride, it's nice to see you."

Cel whispered over to Lock. Who raised her arms and inspected them.

"Is this what I look like as a human?" She mused, a bright smile creeping across her face. I thought, if I had met Lock here, in the fictional realm, as a child, we could have been great friends.

Flora walked till she was right in front of me, Stone close behind, hand on the Boom weapon at his hip. Flora sat, the knees of her crossed legs touching my knees.

"My brother cursed me, Alta."

"We know." I rolled my eyes, and Lock placed a hand on my shoulder to calm me.

"After he did, my fairy grandmother told me how to break the curse. She said, now that I was a mix of fairy and troll, I had to find seven Realmians who were also mixed. Alta, I'm sure you know, mixed races are not common in the Realms. Finding seven of you was a hard task. Stone was the real brains." I felt Lock's hand squeeze as if trying to stop me from saying anything stupid. "HE helped me find my team of mixed Realmians. Thank the suns Lock was traveling with Cel or we might still be searching for the seventh."

"Why seven?" I asked, more harshly than I intended.

"One for each realm and one who was fictional," Flora answered, not saying more.

"Okay… and what are we supposed to do here, in the fictional realm? Just go back?"

"Yes," Flora admitted. Every eye was on her and she offered no explanation.

Pinky stood, anger rising in her eyes, "We traveled all this way, fought fairies, magiced bees, outran a fairy storm and crossed into the fictional realm, just to go back? For nothing?!" She finally screamed at Flora, though she was looking at Stone.

"Well, not completely nothing," Flora announced. "Fairy Grand Mother said that crossing into the fictional realm, with all of you, is what would break my curse…" she looked down at her thin frame, raised her arms for inspection and put them down again. "I'm hoping it'll take effect once we're back through the border?"

"You're HOPE-ing?!" Pinky shouted at her. Stone didn't know what to do. I could see he wanted to step in between them to protect his charge, but Pinky's eyes said, 'don't you move'. But he had a job and moved ever so slightly to cut Flora off from Pinky.

18

T he tiny human is right," the butterfly said from my shoulder. I'd forgotten it was there. "Crossing back over the border always resets you." It continued, "I'll return to being a fairy once I get back. If I can manage it before the madman catches me."

"Right. The guy with the net." Flora said, almost sarcastically. Her being human was creepier than her being a troll. Her voice sounded small and frail, but I knew her as a troll and yet, I could tell it was still her.

"And why did he want to catch you?" Stone asked, still watching Pinky carefully for any sign that it was ok to approach her.

"Wouldn't you want to catch a talking butterfly?" It asked no one in particular. "Ugh, you're all Realmians. Well. Talking animals are not common or even existent at all here. So it's kind of a big deal if you find one... or catch one." It added with a little flutter around the group.

"And why are you a butterfly? Again." Flora asked.

"The boarder changes everyone. All fairies end up as some kind of insect," it said. Every eye turned to Pinky. She was the only other fairy, but neither she nor Flora had turned into insects.

"What?" Pinky shrugged. "She's not one either." She gave a big sweeping arm toward Flora. "Or Alta. I assume it's 'cause we're mixed Realmian races?" The heads bobbed up and down as if considering this for the first time.

"Wait. You two are mixed Realmian races?" The butterfly asked, flitting between Pinky and Flora.

"We all are," Pinky clarified, climbing back onto Blesk. The butterfly dropped in the air an inch as shock stunned his body. He regained his flapping and landed on a blade of grass between Flora and me, still joined at the knee. Flora nodded, I nodded, and the butterfly whistled. Well, he got as close to a whistle as one can with no teeth or lips.

"Ok." Cel broke in, "Is no one else concerned with HOW we are to get back? Alta was right.

No one questions enough on this quest." I swelled with pride, despite trying to stay stoic in the face of human Flora at my knees.

"Settle down there 'leader of the pack'," Wynn interjected.

"I'm pretty glad you're not in the habit of projecting your thoughts to everyone."

"It's actually considered rude to dyri with a large group all at once. Only royals and Beasts of high status do it."

"Diary?"

"Dyri. It's the name for our telepathic communication. Or mindspeak as some realms say."

"Huh, I didn't even think to ask if it had a special name."

"I know. Humans are notoriously simple minded."

"Hey-"

"Sh. Cel is making you proud, remember?"

Cel continued, "Flora, did dear old granny say how to get back?"

Flora shrugged.

"What does that mean?" Cel asked, dropping her arms at her sides. She did her best to hide it, but she was uncomfortable in her fictional realm form. Her skin was still dark but her pointed ears were no longer sticking out from her golden

locks, which weren't golden anymore, but dark
now too, and hung short off her shoulders.

Flora sighed, "Fairy GrandMother didn't tell
me how," she admitted. The group made a
collective sigh, and she continued, "She said the
fictional one would save the day. I trusted her."
She looked back to me and stared.

"Wait. Me?" I shuffled backward and stood.
"How am I supposed to save the day? I don't
know anything about crossing the realms. That's
why you brought Stone." I finished, Flora
watching me, obviously unconvinced.

"I do," the butterfly said. Every head turned
slowly in its direction. "I was hoping to cross
before being caught, but he was too close, and
then there was you guys."

I stared at the butterfly. The chance it was
telling the truth was pretty high. It was a talking
insect in a realm without magic.

"So…" Cel said, trying to coax it out.

"Oh, like, right now? You wanna go now?"

"Of course we want to go now!" Flora
shouted from the grass. Her skin and bones
shaking with annoyance as she rose and
mounted Grable.

"It's pretty easy from this side. No trial by
Crow & Monkey." It rolled its eyes. Or I

imagined it. "So easy, in fact, I'm surprised more Fictionaries don't get through."

"Fictionaries?" Cel asked.

"People from this realm."

"They call themselves that?" Lock asked.

"No. That's what we call them."

"We who? I've never heard that term," Cel was eyeing him suspiciously now.

"Oh. Just some groups I know in the fairy realm, I guess. Shall we?" The butterfly flew up into the air and toward a single tree in the middle of the clearing. It perched on a branch and waited for the rest of the group to mount and make our way to the tree.

"This lone standing tree, in plain sight, is the border to Creomoxxie?" Cel definitely thought her suspicions were on to something now.

"That's what I mean. Yet, no Fictionaries accidentally make it through. Weird, right?" The butterfly continued. "It's like they couldn't find it without a guide."

I wondered who had guided my mother through when she brought me into Creomoxxie. More questions, I sighed.

With everyone under the shade of the tree, the butterfly flittered around the branches and then around the entire tree before landing back on the branch.

Via Dyri

"Are we supposed to do something?" Flora asked. The butterfly just shushed her. Well, it was as close to shushing as an insect with no lips or fingers can manage.

A deafening clatter came from... I looked around. Where? It seemed to echo off every tree in the forest. No. It was coming from the tree. The one we were under now. The clatter clanged and banged as if gears and chains were grinding. Was the border back a draw bridge? Being fictional most of my childhood and in the human realm after, I had little experience with drawbridges, but it seemed to be the kind of sound you knew when you heard it. Even if you'd never heard it before. 'Cause as the sound went on, I was more and more sure of what it was.

Where would a drawbridge even land? Was this a trap? Were we all about to be squished? Wynn's laughter in my brain was loud and strong. If the tree hadn't started growing at that moment, I may have been swayed by the laughter in my head and ended up with a smile on my own face.

The tree expanded upward and outward and the roots rose out of the ground. Roots tangled in-between and around us, rising higher. I was watching as the nearest root grew over my head and swelled. All the raised roots swelled until

148

they touched each other, creating a canopy of roots over the ground and over our heads. Other roots began lowering, closing the space between them, creating a kind of floor? Cel was ducking, Pinky was pulling her weapon. Keenat was tossing his cloak around Erasto, and I could see the magic beginning beneath it. However, there was no need for hiding, fighting, or magical protection. The root ground faded away, the darkness made by the root ceiling dissipated and I saw the great purple sky of Creomoxxie and felt Wynn moving fast under me. The commotion surrounding us made me realize all the unicorns were on the move. As my eyes darted wildly to identify the danger, Wynn shot me a feeling of cold squish and the image of mud.

"Blesk! What's gotten into you?" Pinky hollered.

"We're at the edge of Lake Tylsaa." I hollered, "They're just getting out of the mud."

"The sky. How long were we gone?" Cel asked.

"I'd guess only a few hours. Time in the fictional realm is faster because they're all in a hurry," Stone answered her. Still dodging dirty looks from Pinky.

I felt a hand on my shoulder and spun.

"Lock! Where'd you come from?"

"The fictional realm," she said simply. I smiled.

"I thought someone should know. The madman followed us across the border."

"The who?" I asked, still marveling at our own wonderful sky.

"Not The Who, the madman. He was chasing the butterfly? He followed us through."

My head snapped to Lock, my eyes wide with question. Lock pointed to where the madman was hiding behind a large boulder.

"Where are we?" Asked a sweet, lilting voice. "I don't remember the lake. Where's the tower? And Monkey and Crow?"

My head snapped again toward Flora. She was a fairy. A large one, since we weren't in the fairy realm yet, but still a fairy. Her rough troll skin was now the color of mint ice cream. I hadn't had it since my childhood. There were some things that the fictional realm did right. Ice cream flavors were one of them. Flora's long blue dress flowed down over Grable, making the unicorn look as if it had a long, flowing mane. Her wings fluttered behind her and looked like they had never decided on what to look like. One section was golden and black, like the butterfly we had met. Another section was pale blue and seemed to be made of light. At the top was a section that looked to be just the outline of a wing. Maybe there was a clear membrane? And a furry nest joined the entire visual cacophony between her shoulder blades. Like a very fuzzy moth. I couldn't decide whether I liked them, but they were definitely interesting.

"Did you not expect a fairy?" Wynn asked, amused.

"Kinda, not," I answered with a shrug, then turned to my side. "Lock, monitor the madman. We can assume he doesn't know you're here." I straightened and spoke loudly, "Flora, if this is Lake Tylsaa, which it is," I added to halt any argument. Wynns sense of direction even while trying to avoid the mud, was solid. "Then Tylsaa is just between those mountains." I pointed in front of myself.

"And the fairy realm is four days' ride that way," Stone said, pointing the opposite direction.

"Well, great! Now I have to get all the way home," Flora complained.

"Did you really expect to be dropped into your royal bath chambers?" Pinky asked her. Flora said nothing. "Now that you're a fairy again. I expect we're all ready to be paid," Pinky finished.

"There you all are!" A voice shouted from down the shore. A man was running toward us. Without discussion, the unicorns galloped into place around Flora and their riders pulled weapons to the ready. "Whoa!" He said, slowing to a trot as he approached us. "It's me," he held out his hands as if for inspection. "The butterfly."

"Where are your wings?" I asked quickly, sure I had him caught in his lie. He stared at me and I could feel Wynn groaning in the back of my head.

"I have no wings. No male fairy does." The used-to-be-butterfly man claimed.

"Your Majesty?!!" He shouted, bowing low and staying there. "I beg your pardon. I had no clue it was you in the fictional realm. Please!" He pleaded, "forgive me." Weapons were lowered and unicorns parted back to their spots on the shore. Flora didn't hesitate to respond.

"Rise my subject," she motioned with her hand for him to rise, even though his bow prevented him from seeing it, "and know, you are forgiven. I would not have believed it was me either, and I was the one being her," she ended with a smile.

I marveled again at her regal air and flighty voice. How could a little curse of the body change a being so drastically? Now I understood why Flora was so determined to complete the quest, even if she didn't have all the information, for most of the time. Nope. I suddenly decided.

Someone in line to rule an entire realm should have known to have all the facts before embarking on a quest that endangered the lives of everyone she hired to help her.

Flora was dropping the last bag of payment into the last hand when Keenat shushed the group wildly. He moved around as if listening for a noise only he could hear.

"Drumming. Do you hear it?" He asked no one, still searching for the direction it was coming from. "There," he finally said, pointing off toward the lake.

19

Keenat pointed across the lake. There, in the middle of it, was a ship. I watched as the ship floated toward us. It seemed to pulse on waves in time with the drumming. Each wave pulling the ship closer to the shore. I shook myself out of the trance when Stone whipped past me toward Flora. I joined the others, circling to protect her.

The drumming felt like it was getting closer, but got no louder. A long, thin, orange boat surged toward us. The masts rose out of the hull, tall, and just as I would have expected, except they had flowers where sails should be. Giant pink flowers caught the gusts of wind that pulsed into them with the beat of the drums. Finally, the ship's bow sloshed up onto the mud of the shore in front of us. They shoved a plank from a hole in the side and the end splatted into the mud below.

By unspoken consent, the group, still maintaining our circle around Flora, walked around the ship toward the plank, but back away from its muddied end. The new vantage point gave us a better view of what the plank was for.

People started filing off the ship. They didn't have weapons, armor, or even a scowl among them. I broke the circle and put BoomStick back in Wynn's holster.

"Mother!" Shouted Flora. She had stepped through the opening left by my absence and was now watching the ship with excitement. Those who filed off were taking place at the plank's end. Two rows facing each other, they stood at attention. Finally, as the last footman stepped into place, the one nearest the plank's end raised a trumpet and blew it. The man across from him drummed along, and together they played a quick tune to announce the Fairy Queen.

I first saw her hair as she climbed steps to reach the plank from the ships inside. Her orange locks were piled high and tucked into a sort of hair decoration that looked like intricate lace but gleamed like metal work. A small strand of orange hair fluttered out beside her as she rose out of the ship and onto the plank. Her pale blue, almost white dress hugged her middle and danced about her thick legs like fire licking at a forest. Even without a crown, I knew who this was.

"She has a crown." Wynn chimed in.

"The hair decoration," I answered.

"No. Fairy royals wear a crown around their neck. It shows how they're bound to the land like a leash."

"I don't see a necklace." I said, watching the Queen walk steadily down the plank.

"It's more like a collar. It stands behind her head, ensuring she keeps her eyes on the land and not in the clouds."

I moved my gaze to the Queen's neck, noticing that her loose strands of hair were sparkling. There, sitting around her neck, was a small circlet. But the back of it rose, starting at her shoulders and getting higher as it met at the back of her head. It looked as if the crown I had expected was just backwards and around her neck instead.

"Hmm." I watched it float as the Queen stepped off the plank and into the mud.

"Mother! What are you doing here?" Flora exclaimed, running and throwing her arms around the Queen. "And since when do you have a boat?"

Her mother laughed, and I laughed too as if
commanded by hearing the Queen. I stifled it
quickly and tucked my face into the bag hanging
at Wynn's side.

"My dear Flora. There are so many things
you have yet to learn. Now that you've
completed your pencarian and returned to us. It's
time to begin your training. The Zylphix is in
five days." Flora dropped her mother's hands
and her jaw. "Dear. Pick up your bits. You'll be a
member of the court now. You must act the part
at all times." The Queen finally looked beyond
her daughter and found Stone's eyes. "Stone
GoldWasp. Thank you for assisting my dear one
in her Pencarian," she turned to the entire group,
as if seeing us for the first time. "Thanks be to
all of you. I'm sure that if Flora chose you, it
was for certain reasons, or talents and I'm
thankful you offered them in her service. Each
of you is, of course, invited to Volarmaa for the
Zylphix. You will be our guests until then. If you
wish." With that, she turned, took Flora's hand
and headed back up the plank. She stopped at
the top and turned to address the group again.
"Flora invites those of you interested in traveling
back with us. The boat leaves at first light.
Those wishing to travel with us need only be on
board." The Queen entered the ship, leaving

Flora to descend on her own. She turned to see us and waved her hand wildly.

"Please! Come. I'd love to have you all there, even if you don't join us on the ship. Please find your way to the Zylphix." Everyone nodded and shrugged in response and Flora ducked into the ship.

20

I leaned back to Lock. "How's the madman?"

"Still there. Just hiding behind the tree. Not even hiding well, I might add. If anyone would just look on purpose, they'd see him." I was thankful for Lock's condition. It made the fact that she was sitting backwards on Elgar and blatantly watching the madman, a covert operation in plain sight. I considered what it might take to convince Lock to join me when the group eventually splits up instead of continuing on with Cel.

"Join you where?" Wynn asked. I ignored her cause I had no idea.

"Do we tell Flora?" I said, not really expecting an answer. I looked to the lake and the boat appeared to be sinking. I assumed it was

some kind of magic way it traveled but it didn't
help me in deciding if I should tell Flora about
the madman.

"Hmm," Lock considered it. "Our quest is all
paid up. We're no longer in Flora's employ. Is he
our responsibility? Floras? No ones? I don't
know. He's obviously not the first to come
here." She paused, turning her head to look at
me.

"He might be," I countered.

"How are you half fictional if no one else has
come through?" Lock asked sweetly. I had never
considered that my father might have come to
Creomoxxie. I had always assumed that my
mother went to the fictional realm and met him
there.

"Hmmm," I let the little grunt of
consideration pass my lips so Lock would know
I wasn't upset. "Still, doesn't help us decide."

Music interrupted the quiet of the lakeside. I
assumed it was coming from the ship until Wynn
corrected me. I looked toward the mountains
that separated the lake from its town. Lock
followed my gaze.

"More visitors?" Lock asked, "And the
butterfly fairy took off when the drumming
started."

"Lock. Is there anything you don't see?" I asked her with a smile.

"Nope."

A line of people came over the hill, and music crashed into the valley that housed the lake. Lively, up beat music echoed from the hills. Erasto jumped off Boyle and pulled Keenat down after him, swinging him and dancing around the unicorn.

I motioned Wynn to walk away from Erasto and his dancing spree. She turned slightly, only to smack into by Pinky and Stone.

"Looks like she forgave him." Wynn said, the smile oozing from her voice. I got down and tried to walk away, but Cel was swinging her hips now and even the unicorns were stomping and twisting to the beat.

"I hope this isn't a death march!" I shouted at them. Ignored by all, I moved toward Elgar and rubbed his mane. "Any change?"

"Nope," Lock answered as her foot began tapping by Elgar's side.

"Not you too," I whined.

"Can't help it. The death march has a pretty catchy tune."

The crowd of people got closer, and the music got louder. I tapped along as well and hated my body for betraying me. Wynn was off dancing with Boyle, while Erasto and Keenat continued their way around the entire group.

Why was everyone just standing there, or dancing there, waiting for this mystery party to arrive? Did no one have homes or families to get back to? Was Pinky not ready to be a real fairy again? Were Lock and Cel not ready to resume their own journey? Whatever that was? Wasn't there a hole or cave that Keenat needed to crawl back into?

My head filled with questions, I watched the parade as it came close enough to get a better view. They marched straight toward the lake at first, but now were turning away from me and my group and heading around the far side of the lake. The leader of the parade was a tall person, who wore bright red pants that barely peeked through their obvious dress robe. The colorful frock that draped them heavily was flowing with even more colorful fringe hanging from every spot and made it impossible to tell if they were male or female. Dancers, singers and musicians all followed the leader. Their dusty helmets looking like a lump of dirt atop their heads. The helmet. Dirty. I now saw that many parade walkers were wearing some kind of helmet. Spots, where hands had rubbed them clean as they were donned, shone from so many heads it looked like a river flowing toward the lake.

"It's the Dancing Helmet festival," I finally realized out loud.

"The what?" Shouted Pinky, who was dancing past.

"Dancing Helmet Festival. My mom keeps saying she wants to visit here and see it. It celebrates peace in the human realm by dancing the helmets down to the lake and washing them after another year of not having to use them."

"What a beautiful sentiment." Cel mused as she watched the people parade by. The entire crew stood and watched as the parade died down and made its was along the lake shore. Their muted sound was broken by someone yelling my name, the sound echoing around the lake.

"Alta!" The last person in the parade, the caboose? -was running toward us. They were dressed just like the parade leader, but this person was definitely female. She ran awkwardly as the colored fringe of her robe smacked back and forth with every step. She carried a giant drum across her body and the same dusty helmet as the leader.

"Alta! What in the name of chocolate fudge are you doing here?" The voice said, coming to a panting stop in front of the group that had just collected to protect me. I reveled in it for just a moment. They had moved to protect me, just as they had been doing for Flora.

Via Dyri

What a strange thing for me to be proud of.
"Not really. It means you have friends?"
Wynn interrupted.

"Then why do I also want to scream at all of
them to move?" I asked with as much snark as I
could think at her.

"Cause it means you have friends," Wynn
answered.

"Hello. I'm Amethyst," the caboose said,
taking her helmet off.

"Mom?" I pushed my way through the line
for a better look. "Is that you?"

"Of course, Mom," she started, righting
herself as the panting calmed. "Who else runs
and hollers your name?"

"Flora does, almost daily. I do too,
sometimes. It just comes out, ya know. Alta does
something shocking and amazing and before you
know it, you're shouting her name," Pinky said.
She was milky pink again and her wings
fluttered behind her as she laughed at her own
joke. She stopped quick under Mom's gaze.

"Mom? What are you doing here?" I asked,
finally pushing my way past the circle. She
opened her arms, and I walked right into them.
The 'awww' from behind me reminded me we
weren't alone.

164

"I missed you," she whispered in my ear as I hugged her. She released me and wiped her eyes clear.

"Well, it wasn't a death march," Erasto chimed in, looking from mom to me.

"I've missed you too," I answered, ignoring him and backing up to look mom over again.

"I know. It's the costume I had to wear for the parade. MINT! Chocolate chip. The parade!" She leaned over and scooped up her helmet. "You'll all follow the parade to Tylsaa. Yes? I want to hear all about your adventure. I want to meet the princess!"

"She's out on the boat, Mom." I said then turned to see there was no boat on the lake. Was it still there? Under the depths? How were any of us supposed to get on it if we had wanted to go with them?

"What boat, dear?"

"It's there. In the lake. Like under it," Pinky answered. "It's a Fairy Royal thing."

"Oh, well I'm sure they'd come out- up? If you wanted to meet her."

"That's alright dear," she paused, but then, seeing the helmet in her hand, jumped into action again, trying to make it back to the parade. "Well. The rest of you. Joining us in town? Yes. You are. All of you. Must be tired and hungry. We'll get you all sorted out before bedtime. Promise." She ran back to me, grasped both sides of my face, pulled me forward, and kissed my forehead.

With helmet in hand, Mom rejoined the parade as they filed back past the lake side, making a slight detour at the water's edge to wash her helmet. No good Dancing Helmet Parade leader or caboose, rather, could return with a dusty helmet.

Authors note:

I wrote this entire trilogy using Rory's story cubes as prompts. I was working under the challenge that the "particulars" of any given scene didn't matter. As long as the right information was given at the right time... it mattered little what each scene focused on. Like a parachuter that turned into fancy marriage proposal, a dwarves mushrooms, or a monkey and a crow... I'll admit that one threw me for a loop but it become one of my favorites scenes.

I also admit, a few times I tossed the dice more than once. If the images didn't inspire anything immediately, I gave it another go. I also found quickly that the physical dice I had were not enough for a trilogy. Thankfully the app already existed and I added it to my process.

It was challenging. But also lots of silly fun. It helped to remind me what I was doing in the first place, writing a fantasy story that had fun and heart at its core. Rory's Story Cubes kept my brain light and silly as it forced me to write about a cloaked figure who's best friend was a frog. For that, I'm ever thankful.

I hope you enjoyed seeing how the chapter art played out in each scene. I sure did.

Via Dyri

Acknowledgements

Every book I ever write, that will ever come to fruition, does so with the support of my family. My husband who encourages me daily to keep going, who talks through plot points and helps my characters find their way, often better than I can. My kids for constantly inspiring my stories and for, when necessary, keeping me on task by making me call out how many edits I have left to clear. And my Mom, for cooking all the meals that sustain me and for watching the kids when their interruptions drive me nuts.

My BetaTeam, ARCTeam, and StreetTeam. Creomoxxie is a richer land for your participation. My thanks is endless.

As an Indie author there is nothing more important to me than my readers experience. Please consider leaving a review at StoryGraph.

If you're interested in being 'in the know', joining future Beta, ARC, or Street teams, or just hangin out in the emotionally intelligent group I tend to collect around me; QR it! —>

Persephone Jayne is an emotional intelligence life coach living in New England. She writes emotionally intelligent characters to show readers that such people exist and to, in the most hopeful of cases, be a model of it. She is a retired Navy spouse, homeschools her three kids, and seeks spiritual guidance in nature. She has written almost 10 picture books and 'Creomoxxie Tales' is her first exploration into adult fiction.

@PersephoneJayne

CPSIA information can be obtained
at www.ICGtesting.com
Printed in the USA
BVHW042357270922
648047BV00002B/125

9 781950 460359